"Who _____ Caroline asked then _____

Moyra thought for a few seconds. The answer was as obvious as one of Breddo's riddles. "The dead. Only the dead can fight the dead."

Lady Caroline nodded. "And not just any dead. Only the Knights of the Silver Dragon who died in that long-ago battle with the trolls can fight Nimrae's army. I heard those words from Nimrae's evil lips." She pulled a silver chain out of her bodice, and lifted it off her neck. "I stole this from Father's room early this morning while he was out."

She held up a large silver key at the end of the chain. "This is the key to the crypt where the dead Knights sleep. As the new generation of Knights of the Silver Dragon, you must raise the dead Knights from their dreamless slumber to fight Nimrae's ghost army. Curston depends on you."

Book 1
Secret of the Spiritkeeper

Book 2
Riddle in Stone

Book 3
Sign of the Shapeshifter

Book 4
Eye of Fortune

Book 5
Figure in the Frost

Book 6
Dagger of Doom

Book 7
The Hidden Dragon

Book 8
The Silver Spell

Book 9
Key to the Griffon's Lair

KEY TO THE GRIFFON'S LAIR

CANDICE RANSOM

KNIGHTS
OF THE
SILVER
DRAGON

BOOK 9

COVER & INTERIOR ART
EMILY FIEGENSCHUH

MIRROR STONE

Key to the Griffon's Lair

©2005 Wizards of the Coast, Inc.

Cover and interior art by Emily Fiegenschuh
Cartography by Ted Beargeum
First Printing: October 2005
Library of Congress Catalog Card Number: 2004116882

9 8 7 6 5 4 3 2 1

US ISBN: 0-7869-3827-7
ISBN-13: 978-0-7869-3827-8
620-95017740-001-EN

U.S., CANADA
ASIA, PACIFIC, & LATIN AMERICA
Wizards of the Coast, Inc.
P.O. Box 707
Renton, WA 98057-0707
+1-800-324-6496

EUROPEAN HEADQUARTERS
Hasbro UK Ltd
Caswell Way
Newport, Gwent NP9 0YH
GREAT BRITAIN
Please keep this address for your records

Visit our web site at **www.mirrorstonebooks.com**

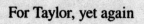

For Taylor, yet again

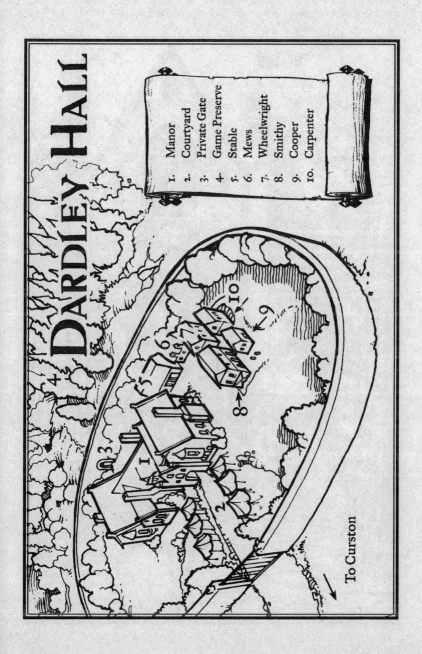

DARDLEY HALL

1. Manor
2. Courtyard
3. Private Gate
4. Game Preserve
5. Stable
6. Mews
7. Wheelwright
8. Smithy
9. Cooper
10. Carpenter

To Curston

CHAPTER

1

Moyra blazed down the Oldgate Highway, well ahead of Driskoll and Kellach.

"Come *on!*" she yelled over her shoulder at the two boys. She had waited all year for this day, and she wasn't about to let her friends slow her down.

The normally locked gates of Dardley Hall stood wide open. About a mile down the road from Curston's Oldgate, the manor house and the lands around it had been owned by the Dardley family for the past fifty years.

Long red banners, emblazoned with griffons, hung from every inch of the stone walls surrounding Dardley Hall. Today was Mop Fair: a once-a-year event when Lord Dardley hired servants for the upcoming hunting season. Visitors from Curston—especially citizens of Broken Town—came in droves, hoping to find work at the stately manor.

With all the people, the courtyard and the surrounding green had turned into a regular party. And Moyra didn't want to miss one moment of the festivities.

She hurried through the gateway. Makeshift vendors' booths, offering food, drink, and trinkets to the job seekers, were scattered throughout the cobblestoned plaza.

Moyra rushed down a row of vendors' booths. She shifted her belt pouch so it wouldn't be jostled by the crowd. She actually had money today. For once, she wouldn't have to steal.

At the first stand, she stopped to finger a hawthorn walking staff. The burnished wood glowed like topaz in the sun. It was nearly as fine as Zendric's gnarled rowan oak crook. With a staff like that and a little magic training, she could cast spells as easily as half-orcs tossed spears.

"Thinkin' of nickin' it? Think again." A leather-faced hunchback scuttled next to her. He gave Moyra a greasy grin, revealing crooked teeth. His only back tooth twinkled.

"Why would I steal your crummy old stick?"

The merchant's breath stank like swamp gas. "I seen you in Curston, filchin' apples and anything else your grubby fingers can swipe. Breddo's girl, ain'tcha? Like father, like daughter."

"You're not fit to wipe my father's boots!" She stomped back toward the courtyard gates.

Moyra felt a hand grip her shoulder. She whipped around, swinging her leg.

She'd teach that slimy hunchback a lesson this time.

Her leg slammed into the stomach of a figure clad in purple wizard's apprentice robes.

"Ow!" Kellach bent over, backing away from her.

His brother, Driskoll, crossed his arms over his chest. "What did you have to do that for?"

Moyra's face flushed. "I'm sorry! I thought . . . I thought you were someone else. Are you okay, Kellach?"

"I'll make it." Kellach gave a weak cough and stood up. "Now, where is this fabulous stall you lured us here for? I'm wearing out my boot leather traipsing after you."

Driskoll eyed a stand filled with sugarcoated cakes. "Can't we get some crumb-buns first? I'm hungry after that race down the highway."

"We can get something to eat after we find the stall." Moyra grabbed Driskoll by the arm. "The lady at this stall sells charms. One-of-a-kind charms. She only comes to Dardley Hall's Mop Fair. I used to come here every year with my granny to buy a charm. But I had white prickles last year, and I missed it."

Driskoll pulled his arm away. "You visited here with your granny? I didn't know you have a grandmother."

"I don't anymore," Moyra said softly. "Thanks to the Sundering. Granny didn't make it."

Though the courtyard teemed with people, a silence fell over the three kids.

Five years ago, fortune hunters had broken the seal in the ruins of nearby Old City. Demons and worse had spewed from the dungeons where they had been locked away. Evil spirits rampaged through Curston, nearly destroying the city which was then called Promise. After the Sundering of the Seal, the city was cursed.

The Sundering had touched every family within Curston's walls. Kellach and Driskoll had lost their mother.

Driskoll looked down awkwardly. "I had no idea your grand-mother had been taken too. I'm sorry."

Moyra pulled on his arm. "You can make it up to me by hurrying *up!*"

She marched the two boys down the row of booths. At last, she pointed. "There! That's her!"

The stall was tended by a pleasant-looking young woman dressed in a blue gown. Her hair was completely covered with a white linen cap. Arrayed on a scrap of velvet were various items in colorful sacks.

"Charms!" the woman called in a clear, ringing voice. "Charms for sale. Cure for the headache! Potion for the heart-sick!"

When Moyra rushed up to the stand, the charm seller stared, transfixed by Moyra's mane of crimson hair. "Red hair, eh? Most unusual."

Driskoll elbowed Moyra. "Red hair must be good luck."

Moyra ignored him. She was too busy gazing at the array of sacks. She knew exactly what she was looking for: something to help her father.

For the past month, her parents had been arguing constantly about her father's line of work. Moyra's father, Breddo, was the worst thief in Curston. He was constantly getting caught in the act of stealing one thing or another. And Moyra's mother was losing patience with him. Moyra thought that if she could find the right charm, her father's luck would turn good again.

"What's this one?" she asked the charm seller. She pointed to a tiny blue sack.

The woman opened the drawstring. A walnut fell onto the velvet. "A spider spins a tiny web inside this shell. Wear it on a thong around your neck and you'll never suffer from toothache again."

Moyra shook her head. "My teeth are fine."

"Ah, perhaps you're looking for something a bit more unusual." The woman selected a crimson sack and pulled out a plain platinum band. "Wear this on your index finger, and no manner of curse or enchantment may harm you."

"That ring reverses spells?" Driskoll was already reaching for his coin pouch. He looked at Moyra and grinned. "I better get this for Kellach's next lesson. Last week, when I showed up to walk him home, he accidentally turned my hair green." Driskoll snickered and held out his coins.

Kellach bridled. "Was it my fault Zendric issued a tripping spell to test my reflexes?"

Moyra laughed, picturing Driskoll with green hair. "Do you have something to give better luck to a thief?" she asked the charm seller.

The woman looked over her shoulder nervously, as if she was watching for someone. "No, but I have something special for you, girl."

The woman bent down. When she straightened up again, she was holding a huge cage draped with a velvet cloth.

"Uh, that's all right." Moyra backed away from the table. "I only have enough coins for a small charm."

"Don't you understand?" the woman asked, reaching out for Moyra's red hair. "You're the one. The red-haired girl with the captain's sons. You must take it. No charge."

She thrust the cage into Moyra's hands.

Moyra pulled back the velvet drapery covering the cage and peered between the golden bars. Inside, a small cream and brown bird clutched a perch. The bird's wings and tail were banded in darker brown. A leather hood topped with a tiny silver bell covered the bird's head, leaving its hooked beak free.

Driskoll and Kellach goggled at Moyra's prize.

"A merlin!" Kellach said, impressed. "A female, unless I miss my guess."

"I can't take this," Moyra said, pushing the cage back into the woman's arms.

"You are the red-haired girl I was told to give this to," she declared. "You must take it!" Her tone left no room for argument.

"But . . ." Moyra groped for words. "I'm not allowed to own a merlin. Only noblewomen and wizards can carry falcons."

6

Four gnomes sauntered up to the stand.

"Go!" the charm seller whispered, shooing Moyra away from the stand. "You must return to Curston. The merlin will lead you. I can say no more." And with that, she turned to her new customers. "Charms! Cure for the headache! Potion for the heartsick!"

Moyra gripped the cage, and together, she and the boys hurried out the courtyard.

"What was that all about?" Kellach asked as they walked down the Oldgate Highway back to Curston.

Moyra shook her head. "I don't know! But no one will believe she just gave this birdcage to me. They'll think I stole it."

They stopped just a few yards outside the Oldgate. Moyra eyed the watchers at the gate and set the cage on the ground.

"What am I going to do?" Moyra asked. "I can't walk through the gate with this bird! If the watchers see me, I'll be the one in a cage! My father's old prison cell!"

A flurry of squawking erupted from the birdcage.

"Moyra, what's wrong with that bird?" Driskoll asked. "It's making an awful racket."

"I'll calm her." Kellach unfastened the cage door. "Zendric's been teaching me a little about falconry. All she needs is a little fresh air." He tried to nudge the merlin off her perch, but the bird's talons dug into his hand. "Ouch!"

He jerked his hand back and sucked on the ragged scratch.

"Maybe the bird doesn't like that hood," Driskoll said. "She can't see."

"That's the point. The hood keeps her calm." Kellach reached into the cage again. "Hey! There's a piece of parchment sticking out of the hood. Maybe that's what's bothering her."

He eased out a miniature scroll. Moyra and Driskoll gathered around as he unrolled it.

Kellach squinted at the tiny ink markings. "It says, 'Follow me to the No Name Pub. Meet the Lone Man.'"

Kellach handed the cage to Moyra. "Ever heard of the No Name Pub?"

She shook her head. "Only the Skinned Cat."

"Where could it be?" Driskoll wondered.

"There's only one way to find out." Moyra untied the hood from the merlin's head. The bird blinked and gave shrill *bik-biks*.

"The charm seller said the merlin would lead us." Moyra nudged the bird's chest until she hopped on her wrist. Slowly she removed her hand from the cage. "All right, bird. Lead on!" The merlin gave a little hop on her fist, then flapped away.

Moyra followed the bird's flight path over the buildings of Curston. "Guess where she's headed?"

Driskoll groaned. "Let me guess. Broken Town."

Moyra grinned. "Your favorite place."

CHAPTER

2

Broken Town lived up to its name. It was a part of Curston that had crumbled under the weight of evil years ago. Even the brightest sun seldom penetrated the darkness that shrouded the winding alleys.

Footpads, petty thieves, beggars, assassins, vagrants, and pickpockets were among the quarter's tamer inhabitants. It was also where Moyra and her family made their home.

Ignoring Driskoll's jumpiness, Moyra followed the flight of the bird, confidently leading her friends down the littered streets. She didn't see anyone, but she sensed a multitude of eyes burning from behind tilted shutters. She knew a person wasn't ever *really* alone in Broken Town.

At last, she came to a stop. Moyra pointed. "I think this is it."

The merlin was circling a pile of bricks and timbers.

No one would ever guess it had once been a building. There didn't even seem to be a door.

"You're kidding," Kellach said.

Moyra put the cage on the ground and opened its door so the merlin could fly back inside. Then she slid feet first into a crack between two crossed timbers. Her hand poked out. "Hand me the cage. And come on!"

Driskoll and Kellach wiggled through the crack behind her. They landed in a damp corridor under the ground.

"Are you *sure* this is right?" Kellach asked. "Where is the barkeep? The tables? The *customers?*"

"They must be here. Somewhere. Trust me." Swinging the cage, she pattered down the dim passageway.

Slate walls oozed grayish green mold. The kids waded in water up to their ankles as they moved down the narrow corridor.

At last, they arrived at a small wooden door laced with spiderwebs.

"This must be it," Driskoll said. He batted away a sticky cobweb covering the door handle.

The web's owner, a large brown spider marked with an orange bull's-eye, skittered down a thread. It leaped on Driskoll's head.

"Yikes!" Driskoll yelped. Kellach swatted the spider to the floor.

Moyra didn't wait for the boys. She pushed the door open and stepped into the room. Wide maple planks lined the floor.

On the walls, everburning torches guttered in blackened sconces. A ramshackle counter stood in one corner. The barkeep, who didn't even glance in their direction, was pulling a pint for a man dressed all in black. Two other men sat sullenly around rickety tables. They glared at Moyra through a haze of pipe smoke, but they did not say a word.

"Now what?" Driskoll whispered once he and Kellach had caught up to her. "Which one is our man?"

Moyra marched up to the barkeep and held up the golden cage. "I'm looking for—"

Before she could finish, he jerked his thumb toward an arched doorway in the back.

Moyra hurried across the scuffed wooden floor, trying not to meet the gaze of the swarthy guests. Driskoll and Kellach scuttered behind her.

In the back room, she saw a figure at the single table, lit by a flickering candle. The man's clothes made the other pub crawlers look like guests at Dardley Hall.

His leggings were ripped and stained with what looked like dried blood. The handle of a wicked dagger poked out of one cracked boot.

Most of the stranger's body was completely swathed in a hooded cloak, so dusty it looked as if he'd been on the road for weeks. His face was hidden.

Moyra cleared her throat. She lifted up the birdcage. "Excuse me, sir. Did you send for me? For us?"

The stranger nodded slowly, then flung back the hood of the great cloak.

Moyra gaped in astonishment.

CHAPTER

3

Freed from the hood, the stranger's butter-colored hair rippled to her waist. The smoking taper on the table cast soft shadows on her heart-shaped face. But lines of worry creased her forehead, and her dark blue eyes were serious.

"You—you're a girl!" Driskoll stammered.

The blond girl arched a fair eyebrow. "If the fate of Curston rests on someone with such keen perception, we are indeed doomed." Her voice carried more amusement than sarcasm.

"The fate of Curston?" Driskoll asked. "What is this about?"

"Please, sit," said the girl. "Let me explain."

Driskoll and Moyra took seats at the table. Moyra pushed the birdcage across the table. "Here. I believe this is yours."

The girl peered into the cage with a gentle smile, then looked back at Moyra. "Thank you for taking care of my bird."

Kellach pulled out one of the rickety wooden chairs and sat down. "Are you in danger, Lady Dardley?"

The girl's eyes widened. "How do you know who I am?"

"I've seen you before," Kellach replied matter-of-factly. "Several months ago, I went with my father to Dardley Hall. Lord Dardley was planning a big feast and wanted to hire an off-duty watcher. My father is Torin, captain of the watch."

"Yes, I know," said the girl. "I remember your visit. I was sitting by the fire with my maid, plying my embroidery needle like any good daughter of the manor while you spoke with my father. I'm surprised you noticed me at all."

Kellach grinned triumphantly. "I notice almost everything."

Moyra rolled her eyes at Driskoll, then turned back to the girl. "If you're Lady Dardley, what are you doing in this weird tavern?" Moyra pointed at the girl's torn tights and her dirty cloak. "And why are you dressed like that?"

"It's not easy for the daughter of Dardley Hall to sneak away into the walls of Curston," the girl explained. "But even with the commotion of the Mop Fair, it wasn't safe for us to speak there. I chose this disguise so I could walk out of the manor house and through the gates of Curston without anyone recognizing me. You see,"—she clasped her hands together tightly as if she were praying—"I'm desperate. I know you are Knights of the Silver Dragon, and I need your help."

"We Knights are at your service, Lady Dardley." Driskoll bowed his head.

The girl laughed. "Thank you. But please call me Lady Caroline. We're going to know each other quite well before this is all over." She looked over her shoulder, then continued. "I'm sorry we had to meet in a place such as this, but secrecy is of the utmost importance. I'm in danger. We *all* are. Every citizen in Curston is in terrible danger."

"Danger?" Moyra felt the fine hairs along her arms crawl. "What kind of danger?"

The girl shook her head imperceptibly. "Shhh. We must speak softly. Though this is the safest place in Curston for me to speak freely, the walls have ears."

Moyra, Kellach, and Driskoll all looked at her expectantly.

"Let me explain." Lady Caroline took a deep breath, then plunged into her story. "You see, the anniversary of my grandfather's death is three days from today. My grandfather was the first Lord Dardley."

Kellach nodded. "I've heard of him. The first Lord Dardley was one of the legendary Knights of the Silver Dragon."

"Was your grandfather killed in the Sundering?" Moyra asked.

Lady Caroline shook her head. "He died fighting in the Troll Invasion, just before the Sundering. But my father believes Grandfather was murdered in the foulest way. And that the murderer is"—Lady Dardley leaned forward, placing her hands flat on the table—"Zendric."

15

Moyra gasped. "Zendric? That's crazy! Zendric is a wise and kind wizard. I know he would never murder anyone."

Lady Caroline's forehead creased with worry. "I know that too. But my father swears Zendric killed Grandfather."

"How exactly was he killed?" Driskoll asked.

Lady Caroline bit her bottom lip. "He was beheaded."

Moyra gulped. She didn't know what to say. None of them did. In the silence that followed, Moyra could hear water dripping from somewhere at the back of the little room. A slow drip, drip, drip, like blood from—

She blinked to banish the gory image that popped into her mind.

"Your father must be mistaken." Driskoll crossed his arms. "Zendric would never behead anyone. He probably used magic to kill your—"

Moyra poked Driskoll in the ribs and gave him a hard look. "How could you even assume Zendric actually hurt Lady Caroline's grandfather! He would never kill a fellow Knight!"

"Moyra's right. This doesn't sound like Zendric." Kellach turned to Lady Caroline. "Why does Lord Dardley believe this? Was he there when—when it happened?"

"He was away on a quest and didn't learn the news until after the funeral." Lady Caroline lowered her voice. "But he saw my grandfather's murder in a vision a few months ago."

"Did he dream the vision?" Driskoll asked. "I have strange dreams sometimes."

"He saw it in a basin of water," replied Lady Caroline.

"This is ridiculous!" Moyra slammed her fist down on the table. "Your father is accusing Zendric of cold-blooded murder because he saw something in his *washbasin*?"

"I didn't say a washbasin," Lady Caroline said calmly. "My father saw the image in a basin brought to him by Nimrae, our house wizard."

"House wizard? What's that?" asked Driskoll.

"It's one of the privileges of owning an estate," answered Lady Caroline. "My father has all manner of servants, maids, marshals, and staff to run Dardley Hall. Normally, he only takes on new staff at the Mop Fair. But this year, he hired a new servant months in advance of the fair—Nimrae, the house wizard. That's when all the trouble began." Lady Caroline sighed. "Father began confiding in Nimrae about our family's past. Then last week, Nimrae brought the basin. When my father saw the vision, he vowed to destroy Zendric."

Moyra threw up her hands. "So, you're asking us to help your father seek revenge on Zendric? We would never do anything to betray Zendric. He is *not* a murderer! Come on, boys! Let's get out of here." She stood up and turned toward the doorway.

Lady Caroline grabbed her arm. "Wait! Please!" she shouted, breaking her own rule. "I never said I believed Zendric was a murderer. I said that is what my *father* believes." She leaned forward again and looked earnestly into Moyra's face. "I don't want you to help me hurt Zendric. I want you to help me save him. You are the only ones who can help me, help *all* of us. Please believe me."

Kellach tilted his head at Moyra. "Give her a chance to finish her story at least."

Moyra sighed and returned to her seat.

"Forgive me. I know I sound like a lunatic, babbling on about visions in washbasins." Lady Caroline wrung her white hands. "It sounds strange even to me. I never imagined that something such as this would blacken the Dardley name. My father has always been a kind, fair, and just man. But I don't know what or who he is anymore. Ever since Nimrae came, he's changed."

Kellach leaned forward. "Are you saying Nimrae has put a spell on Lord Dardley?"

Lady Caroline's eyes expressed bottomless sadness. "I'm not sure. Whatever it is, Nimrae seems to control him more and more each day."

"So, what does your father plan to do?" Moyra asked. "Zendric is the most powerful wizard in Curston. It will be difficult to destroy him, to say the least."

"True, it won't be easy." Lady Caroline nodded. "But Nimrae is a clever wizard in his own right. He knows he can't kill Zendric outright. Zendric is too strong for that. Instead, Nimrae convinced my father to destroy the one thing Zendric loves more than anything . . . the city of Curston."

Driskoll's eyes grew wide. "How?"

"Nimrae has conjured an army of ghosts in a secret laboratory.

18

On the anniversary of my grandfather's death, Nimrae plans to order the undead army to destroy Curston and everyone in it. Destroying the city will be the ultimate revenge."

"How do you know all this?" asked Kellach. "Did Lord Dardley tell you?"

"Of course not!" Lady Caroline gave an unladylike snort. "My father still sees me as a child. He doesn't realize I'm nearly seventeen." Lady Caroline brushed back her long hair. "Nimrae counsels my father every evening after supper. Last night, I positioned myself behind a pillar in the great hall, near my father's private chamber, and I heard Nimrae explain the entire plan."

"How do you know the army is real, though?" Kellach asked. "Nimrae could be lying to your father."

"I wish he were." Lady Caroline's blue eyes reflected remembered terror. "But I know for a fact he's not. I saw one of his . . . creations myself last night."

Driskoll's jaw went slack. "You saw a ghost?"

She nodded. "Nimrae gave my father a demonstration. He conjured a man dressed in armor, armed to kill. A man with no emotions, no soul, ice water in his veins. I was never so frightened in my life. Nimrae told my father he had a hundred of those killing machines ready to move at his signal."

Moyra let the image sink in. Then she said quietly, "So how can we stop them? A ghost army created by a wizard sounds invincible to me."

"I know." Lady Caroline looked down at her hands for a moment. Then she looked back up, her eyes glistening. "But there is hope. I realized last night Nimrae's army is not all-powerful. There is one way it can be destroyed."

"How?" Moyra and Driskoll asked at the same time.

"Who do you think can battle the dead?" Lady Caroline asked them.

Moyra thought for a few seconds. The answer was as obvious as one of Breddo's riddles. "The dead. Only the dead can fight the dead."

Lady Caroline nodded. "And not just any dead. Only the Knights of the Silver Dragon who died in that long-ago battle with the trolls can fight Nimrae's army. I heard those words from Nimrae's evil lips." She pulled a silver chain out of her bodice, and lifted it off her neck. "I stole this from Father's room early this morning while he was out."

She held up a large silver key at the end of the chain. "This is the key to the crypt where the dead Knights sleep. As the new generation of Knights of the Silver Dragon, you must raise the dead Knights from their dreamless slumber to fight Nimrae's ghost army. Curston depends on you."

In her cage on the table, the merlin gave a small *bik-bik*.

Driskoll gulped. "Excuse me, Lady Caroline, we don't know *how* to raise the dead."

"I'll find a way," Kellach said confidently. "We've faced down bigger foes than a bunch of ghosts."

"Assuming we can figure out a way to raise the dead," Moyra said, "where can we find the crypt?"

"I'm afraid I don't know," Lady Caroline said. "The crypt is said to be marked with a griffon like this." She pointed at the creature engraved on one side of the key: Its body looked like a muscular lion's. Its head and front legs looked like an eagle's. Out of its back sprouted two enormous wings.

She turned the key over. On the other side was an odd pattern, a small circle with many spokes radiating out of it, like a stylized sun. "I believe this circular symbol is a clue to the crypt's location."

"You have *no* idea where we'll find the crypt?" Moyra pressed. "This will be like hunting for the Lost Gold of Curston." According to legend, the city's treasure had mysteriously disappeared during the Sundering.

Lady Caroline smiled. "I have heard stories of your exploits, Knights of the Silver Dragon. Even though most of Curston sees you as mere children, I know that you are heroes in your own right. If anyone can find the crypt and raise the Knights, you three can. Please. Will you help?"

Moyra released a sigh. She looked at Kellach and Driskoll. "Shall we put it to a Silver Dragon vote?"

Kellach nodded. "All in favor?" All three kids raised their hands.

"It's settled then," Kellach said. "We'll help."

Lady Caroline pressed the silver key into Kellach's palm.

"Godspeed."

As Kellach wrapped his fingers around the key, Lady Caroline gave a little gasp. A long red welt marked the skin on his index finger.

She looked at the birdcage on the table, then back at Kellach. "You got in the way of the merlin?"

Kellach pulled back his hand. "Yes. But it's just a scratch. I'll be all right."

Lady Caroline drew a pouch from her sash and brought out a small vial. "I apologize for my bird. She can be vicious when she has a mission to accomplish." She pulled the cork out of the vial. "This salve should take the fire from your wound."

After she had smeared the lotion on Kellach's wound, Lady Caroline rose and grabbed the merlin cage from the table. "Remember. I will be your ears at Dardley Hall. If I learn anything new, I will send my merlin. Tell no one that you've seen me here. Nimrae's spies are everywhere. The only one you can trust is Mary, my maid."

"How will we know your maid?" Moyra asked.

"You've already met her. She was the charm seller who gave you my merlin."

Moyra gaped. "Your maid is the charm seller?"

"Mary was once a Traveler. I hired her after meeting her at the Mop Fair one year. She's taught me everything I know about the healing arts.

"Now go!" Lady Caroline pushed them toward the doorway. "You must hurry! And please . . . be careful!"

In a solemn line, Moyra, Kellach, and Driskoll passed through the main tavern room. The tables were still occupied by the same men. The barkeep was polishing steins.

Going back through the pub was eerier than entering it. Patches of dark green mildew grew thicker than dwarves' beards on the walls. The stale air felt heavy, swaddling them like a wet blanket and making it difficult for them to lift their feet.

"I feel like I'm walking through ghosts," Kellach said. "Like I'm passing through the shades of people who lived here a century ago."

"I think you have ghosts on the brain," his brother said.

"Who wouldn't after that story?" Kellach asked.

"Didn't you think it was odd," Moyra said, "that Lady Caroline would meet us here? How would someone like her even know about this place? I've never heard of this pub before, and I *live* here."

"Shhh," Driskoll said, as he opened the door back into the small corridor. "Remember? Nimrae's spies are everywhere. Let's talk when we're out of here."

They walked back up the slanting passage in silence and scrabbled through the crack in the crossed timbers.

They stood in the alley for a long moment, staring at each other.

"Now what?" asked Driskoll, brushing off his already dirty jacket. "Where do we start looking for a crypt full of dead Knights?"

"Shhh!" Moyra tilted her head. "Before we start looking for dead Knights, I think we'd better deal with whomever—or whatever—is watching us!"

CHAPTER

4

Driskoll whipped around but saw no one. "How do you know someone is watching us?"

"I'm from here, remember?" Moyra said. "If you want to stay alive in Broken Town, you develop good hearing."

Kellach listened. "I don't hear anything unusual. At least, not unusual for Broken Town."

Moyra focused on the sound. She heard a soft *pad-pad* coming from behind them. It was growing closer.

"I hear it," whispered Driskoll. "It sounds like heavy paws. Like a big dog—" He didn't finish his sentence.

The padding sound grew closer.

"Don't turn around!" Moyra warned the boys. "Just—"

The *pad-pad* stopped behind them. Moyra sensed the creature's muscles tensing, as if it was preparing to leap.

"Run!" Moyra shrieked.

The three kids tore out of the alley. Moyra felt a rush of

wind pushing at her back, as if the very air had gathered itself into a vengeful force. No one turned to look at the pursuer. Even that small motion would slow them down and put them closer to deadly jaws.

Moyra sprinted out of the alley, down the street, and careened around the corner so fast her red hair streamed behind her like a banner. Kellach stuck close to her heels, but Driskoll trailed last.

"Hurry!" she told Driskoll, risking a quick glance over her shoulder. She sensed rather than saw a vast whiteness, as if they were trapped in a sudden blizzard. Inside the blizzard an enormous shape formed, disintegrated, and re-formed.

"Kell!" she yelled. "Can you throw a spell on this thing?"

She felt a hot, moist breath on the back of her neck—a heat as strong as a roaring cooking fire.

"Of course! Just give me a moment—" Kellach kept running, but his lips moved in a silent litany.

She suspected Kellach was mentally sifting through his repertoire of magical abilities. Simple spells would be useless against a beast that size. The more complex spells would take too long. The three of them would be supper before Kellach could conjure a blocking spell or hurl a magical weapon at the creature.

Moyra skidded in front of a dilapidated building.

"This way!" she cried.

She kicked the glass out of a small basement window with

her boot, then dived through an opening barely large enough for her narrow hips.

Kellach slipped through next, the jagged glass straining against his much bigger figure. He dropped to the floor and dusted off his purple apprentice robes.

"That was close," he said, turning away from the window. "I almost—"

A pair of feet poked through the window, kicking him in the head. "Ow! Driskoll! That's my head."

The rest of Driskoll's body vaulted through the window.

"Sorry!" Driskoll said, picking himself off the dirty floor. "I didn't see you there."

Moyra stared up at the window expecting the white fury to smash through the flimsy casing and land on them—claws curved and teeth bared like the shards of glass still in the frame.

But nothing appeared at the window except a faint ray of late afternoon sun.

"It's—it's gone!" she said in astonishment.

"What *was* that thing?" Driskoll asked.

"Most likely a figment of our collective imagination," Kellach said.

"Speak Common, or I'll kick you again," Driskoll said.

"I'm saying that weird pub could have made us imagine anything. None of it seemed real." Kellach gave an exaggerated shudder. "I could swear I was walking through the ghosts of former customers."

Driskoll gazed around the grubby basement. "Where are we?"

"In an old warehouse," Moyra said. "I know the way out. But we could use a little light."

"Allow me." Kellach whipped a thin iron rod out of his robes. He tapped it against the floor, and a bright light erupted from its golden tip.

"You coming?" Driskoll asked Moyra, who was still sitting on the floor. "Or do you want us to leave without you?"

"You couldn't crawl out of a gopher hole without my help," she said. "Just hang on a moment. I've got something stuck to my boot."

Moyra turned back to stare at the bottom of her right boot. She plucked the object from the sole and examined it in the half-light from the window. It was a tuft of white fur, long and silky.

"Look!" she said. "Do figments have fur?"

Kellach ran two fingers along the length of the tuft. "Too long to be from a house cat."

"And too clean," Moyra added as she scrambled to her feet. "Even a white cat in Broken Town would be gray."

"Maybe Zendric would know where the fur came from," Driskoll suggested as they ducked past a stack of crates. "We should ask him."

"I don't know," Moyra said as she led the boys through the warehouse. Large double doors loomed before her, secured with a thick metal bar. She lifted the bar and set it against the wall.

"Lady Caroline told us not to tell anyone we'd been to the No Name Pub," Moyra continued. "If we show Zendric the fur, we'll have to explain where we got it, and then we'll have to tell him about what Lady Caroline said. Are you sure that's a good idea?"

"I know what Lady Caroline said, and I know she didn't mean Zendric." Kellach heaved his weight against the wooden doors. They flung open without a squeak. "Zendric's a Knight too, remember? He'll tell us where we can find the old Knights' crypt. If we warn him about Nimrae's plans, maybe he can stop Nimrae in his tracks before any of this even gets started."

Moyra looked at Kellach. Somehow she knew it wouldn't be quite that easy.

■ ■ ▊ ■ ▊

The Wizards' Quarter, on the east side of the city, was as different from Broken Town as chalk from cheese. Moyra breathed deeply. Instead of the stink of garbage, the air here held the scent of fragrant spell-casting potions.

They passed a shop called Wizard Wares. Moyra stopped for a moment to admire an emerald-knobbed staff, but she was particularly taken by an ermine robe. Embroidered crescent moons and stars swirled around the matching hat, mimicking the night sky as it progressed through the seasons. If only she had a little of that power . . . she had no desire to rule Curston, like Lord Dardley and Nimrae, only to make life better for her family.

They turned onto the street where Zendric lived. Zendric's tower rose above the smaller houses.

Kellach opened the coiled metal gate. As they strode through Zendric's small garden, Moyra recognized the plants Zendric grew for his potions and enchantments. She saw roses, white violets, and pale pink laurel before she reached the stairs to Zendric's door.

Kellach reached out to knock on the door. But it swung open, unlocked. He frowned and looked over his shoulder at Moyra. "That's strange. Zendric is never this careless." He poked his head inside. "Zendric? Are you here?"

No reply.

"He's not home," Moyra said. "Let's go."

"I'll close the door. I don't feel right leaving it open." Kellach started to pull it shut when Moyra stopped him.

"Wait," she said. "What was that?"

"What?" Kellach asked.

But Moyra's sharp ears picked up the faint sound.

"Don't leave!"

"It's Zendric!" she said. "He's in there, all right."

The kids hurried into the main room but did not see the wizard.

"Zendric?" Kellach called. "Where are you?"

"Up here."

"Hurry!" Moyra said. "It sounds like Zendric is in trouble!"

CHAPTER

5

Moyra thudded across the main tower room and up the wooden staircase to Zendric's study, followed by Driskoll and Kellach. The room was never neat, but now it looked as if all the half-orcs in Curston had had a party in it.

The wooden desk under the window was piled with spell-books. Powdery substances spilled from tipped mortars. Snake skins, soiled robes, pointy hats, and all sorts of magical items lay strewn on the floor and under one of the armchairs—an armchair that was occupied by Zendric himself.

The wizard lay motionless against the leather cushions. His face was a lighter shade of gray than his beard.

"Zendric!" Kellach rushed to his side. "What's the matter? Are you sick?"

"Just a dizzy spell." The elderly wizard flapped his hand carelessly, and struggled to get up.

Kellach exchanged a concerned glance with Moyra.

"What's wrong, Zendric?" he asked. "I've never seen you with a cold, much less so ill you can't get up out of a chair."

Moyra put her hand on Zendric's arm. "Have you come down with the white prickles? I had them at this time last year—"

"No, no. Nothing like that. It's . . . just old age," Zendric replied, his voice gaining strength with each word. He looked up at Kellach. "You've already had your lesson this morning. What are you doing here?"

"We came to ask you about Nimrae," Kellach said.

"Nimrae?" Zendric's bushy eyebrows rose in surprise. "How do you know about him?"

"We all heard about him from Lady Caroline—Lady Dardley," Driskoll said. "We met her at the No Name Pub in Broken Town. We just came from there."

If Zendric's eyebrows lifted any higher, they would take flight. "Lady Dardley met *you* three in the most disreputable pub in Curston? In Cuthbert's name, *why*?"

"She asked us to," said Kellach.

Zendric's eyebrows—which seemed to have a life of their own—shot downward in anger. "Are you going to make me drag the story out of you three, syllable by syllable, or will someone tell me what is going on?"

"Lady Caroline told us Lord Dardley saw a vision—that you killed his father in the Troll Invasion," said Kellach.

Moyra wasn't sure whether it was a good idea to involve

Zendric, but now that the boys had explained so much, there was no point in holding back.

She told Zendric everything, exactly as Lady Caroline had explained it to them. "And so," Moyra finished, "she called on us because we are the new Knights of the Silver Dragon. We only have three days to locate the crypt and raise the dead Knights to fight Nimrae's ghost army."

Zendric pushed against the chair, struggling to his feet. He leaned heavily against the armrest. He turned to Moyra. "Quickly, child, hand me my staff. Your favorite, with the stone that resembles your face."

Moyra picked out a rowan oak crook from the earthen jar filled with canes and staffs by the door. It had a reddish, stone carved with a young girl's features.

Gripping the sturdy staff, Zendric hobbled over to the desk under the window. Stacks of spellbooks were scattered across its surface, and vials filled with colorful potions sat in a neat row along the windowsill. The old wizard picked up the vials of potions, one by one, examining their yellowed labels.

"I sensed something like this might come to pass," Zendric said. "Nimrae paid me a visit last week. He has Lord Dardley dancing on the end of a string, believing I killed his father— Aha!"

Zendric uncorked a vial, tipped his head back, and emptied the contents into his mouth. He wiped his lips with the edge of his robe, then continued, "Dardley has had a whiff of blood—thanks to his 'house wizard'—and will stop at nothing to see his father's death avenged."

"That's what Lady Caroline said," Kellach said. "She doesn't believe you killed her grandfather. She thinks Nimrae might have cast a spell over her father's mind, making him want to destroy Curston. Do you think she's telling the truth?"

"You can trust Lady Caroline. I've known her since the day she was born." Zendric coughed weakly. "If she says that Nimrae is influencing Lord Dardley, you can believe her. That wizard is more dangerous than a half-orc with a headache." He paused, then added soberly, "It's no accident he's at Dardley Hall. He's staking out Curston because he wants something—something he can't conjure. And he needs me out of the way to get it."

"Did Nimrae cast a spell on you?" asked Driskoll.

Zendric nodded. "He tried. But I shut him out. So he must have hatched this new plan instead. You said Nimrae plans to raise his ghost army in three days' time?"

Zendric hobbled over to the bookcase. He removed a dusty leather-bound volume. "We'll need every second to locate the crypt. From what I understand, it's quite well hidden."

Kellach's face fell. "Wait. You mean, you don't know where it is?"

Zendric turned back and glared at Kellach. "Believe it or not, boy, I am not privy to every single matter in Curston. Secrets exist that even I don't know about." The wizard's expression softened. "Did Lady Caroline have any clue about where we might find the crypt?"

Kellach hung his head. "Not exactly. But she gave us this." Kellach pulled the silver key from his pocket. "The griffon on this side matches the griffon that marks the crypt." Kellach flipped it over. "She said these marks on the other side may be a clue to the crypt's location. Do you recognize it?"

"Hmm, let me see that, boy." Zendric reached to take the key from Kellach, leaning heavily on his staff. But the hand gripping the staff shook so violently that he couldn't keep his balance. The old wizard's eyelids fluttered, and he tumbled to the floor.

"Zendric!" Kellach rushed to his side.

Zendric groaned and rolled over. "I'm all right, lad. Just another . . . dizzy spell."

"Let us help you." Kellach took one of the wizard's arms. "Driskoll, Moyra, get on his other side."

Together they lifted Zendric across the room and back to the leather armchair.

"Much better," Zendric said with obvious relief. "Just let me rest here a moment, and we can begin our search for the crypt."

Kellach exchanged another concerned glance with Moyra and Driskoll. "Are you sure? You look terrible."

Moyra thought Zendric would anger at Kellach's words, but instead the elderly wizard seemed to crumple, collapsing like an empty waterskin.

When Zendric spoke, his voice was distant and weary. "Perhaps you're right, my lad. You three begin without me. After I take a short nap, I'll join you." Zendric leaned back against the armchair, his eyes half-closed.

Driskoll shook Zendric's shoulder softly. "Wait! Don't fall asleep yet. Lady Caroline warned us to watch out for Nimrae, but we've never seen him. What does he look like?"

"He can be . . . anyone . . . anywhere," Zendric said slowly.

"He's a shapeshifter?" Driskoll asked.

"No." Zendric struggled to sit up in his chair. His face regained a bit of color, but his voice was still soft and weak. "He's a master of disguise. He also has a familiar."

"Like Locky?" Driskoll asked. Locky was Kellach's familiar, a small clockwork dragon that had been created by a friend of Zendric's not long after they'd all been made Knights of the Silver Dragon.

"Similar. But Nimrae's familiar is a living, breathing animal—a goshawk."

"A goshawk?" asked Driskoll. "What's that?"

Zendric spoke with his eyes closed, and his words were slightly slurred. "Large . . . gray . . . hawk."

Moyra stepped forward. "But how will we know Nimrae if we meet him?"

"Only . . . one way. . . He . . . has no shadow." And with that, Zendric's head drooped against his chest, and he began to snore.

Moyra felt a lump in her throat. They had faced enemies without Zendric before, but none as clever and powerful as Nimrae. Even with Kellach's talents, she was afraid they had met their match.

"We'd better go," Kellach whispered. He backed up, motioning to Moyra and Driskoll to follow him. Without another word, they tiptoed down the stairs, across the main tower room, and out the door.

Just as Kellach pulled Zendric's gate shut, Driskoll's eyes flew wide. "Oh no! We forgot to ask Zendric about the fur Moyra found on her boot."

Kellach fastened the latch. "We don't have time to worry about that now. We're supposed to be hunting for the crypt, remember? We have less than three days to find the crypt and somehow raise the dead Knights to battle Nimrae's army." He held up the silver key. "Before we do anything, we need to figure out the symbol on the back of this key. Lady Caroline believed it was a clue."

Driskoll scuffed the toe of his boot against the cobblestone. "But where do we start?"

Moyra chewed the skin around her thumbnail. Lady Caroline had sent her maid, Mary, to give Moyra the merlin. Lady Caroline was counting on her—on them. If she and the boys didn't succeed in stopping Nimrae's army, it would be like the Sundering all over again. Moyra thought of her granny and how she had fought so valiantly that day.

She gasped. Of course!

"Boys! My granny had a friend. A Traveler like Mary. Rom knows all sorts of things. The Old Ways, everything. He might remember the Troll Invasion and know about the Knights."

Kellach snorted. "I thought you didn't want to tell anyone about Nimrae and the ghost army!" He put on a mocking, singsong voice. "Lady Caroline told us not to tell anyone we'd been—"

Moyra slugged him in the arm. "We can trust Rom. Believe me." She put her fists on her hips. "And he might be able to help us in a way even Zendric can't."

"What do you mean?" Driskoll asked.

Moyra turned serious. "You'll see."

Kellach sighed. "Well, I guess it's worth a try. So how do we find this Rom person? Don't Travelers live outside Curston?"

"Not Rom. He decided to come inside the city walls after the Sundering. Granny left her house to him."

Driskoll groaned. "Don't tell me. He lives in Broken Town."

Moyra grinned. "Where else?"

CHAPTER

6

"Why did Rom give up traveling and settle in Curston?" Kellach asked as they picked their way down cluttered alleys of Broken Town.

"Yeah," said Driskoll. "I wouldn't mind traveling the world, living in a red and yellow wagon."

"I think he got tired of all the fighting," Moyra answered. "Since the Sundering, even Travelers aren't safe."

Driskoll's interest perked up. "Has Rom ever been to Deeping Well? I've heard that anyone who gazes into the bottomless waters of the Well will have the gift to see Beyond." He added wistfully, "I wouldn't mind having that ability."

Moyra marched up to the wooden door of a tidy cottage and rapped.

"This little house is far too tame for a wild Traveler," Kellach remarked.

"Don't be fooled by the heartsease in the garden." She raised her hand to knock again, but the door swung inward.

The biggest man any of them had ever seen loomed over them. His massive shoulders filled the doorway. His hair and beard were blacker than a raven's feathers. Thick brows bridged his beaky nose in a perpetual scowl.

"Rom, it's me!" Moyra shouted.

The man's face split into a wide, gap-toothed grin.

"Chavi!" he cried in a booming voice. With one stout arm, he scooped her up into a smothering embrace.

Moyra wriggled away. "Rom!" she protested. "I'm not five years old anymore."

"To me, you will always be my little Chavi tagging after your *Kokko* Rom." Tousling her hair, he stepped back. "Come in. Who have you brought to see me? I don't have many guests these days."

"These are my friends, Kellach and Driskoll," Moyra said. "Torin's sons."

Rom grinned. "Torin's sons, eh? *Gavver.*"

"What?" Driskoll asked.

Kellach bristled. "What's wrong with being a watcher? My father is good at his job."

Rom nodded at Kellach. "You understand the tongue of Travelers, eh? I will have to be careful of what I say."

"Kellach is an apprentice wizard," Moyra explained. "He understands many languages."

Rom gave Moyra an exaggerated wink. "Are you planning

to throw the cake over the hedge for this young man?"

Moyra blushed to the roots of her hair. "Rom! I'm only thirteen! Anyway, I'm not *ever* going to throw a cake over the hedge."

"*What* are you all talking about?" Driskoll said, clearly tired of hearing everyone speaking in riddles. "Why would anybody throw a perfectly good cake in the woods?"

Rom exploded with laughter, putting his arm around Driskoll's shoulder. "Come sit down. I'll give you some of my special tea and explain Traveler ways."

The inside of the cottage was as cozy as a house in a child's storybook. An open stained-glass window let in the evening breeze. A fire in the hearth bathed the single room in warm light. A pot on an iron tripod was suspended over the crackling flames. In front of the hearth sat a worn, patterned rug. A cot made up with a red and yellow patchwork blanket stood under the window, and a plain wooden table filled the center of the room.

The house did not look like the home of a dark-eyed giant.

Moyra read Driskoll's and Kellach's curious stares. "Rom didn't change anything in my granny's house."

"Who does not like comfort? Sit, sit," Rom said, pulling out several roughhewn stools from underneath the old table.

Driskoll plunked himself down on one and scooted it closer to the fire. "Now, what's this about throwing away a cake?"

Rom laughed again. "When a girl likes a boy, she throws a cake baked with coins inside over the hedge to him. It means she wants to marry him."

"Moyra throw coins away? Never!" Kellach laughed.

"Rom—" Moyra rolled her eyes.

The big man crept over to the fire. He pulled several mugs out of a cupboard above the hearth and filled them with liquid from the pot. Rom handed a mug to each of his guests, then pulled up a stool next to Moyra.

"Now, you didn't come here to discuss Traveler ways, did you?" Rom turned to Moyra. "What is on your mind, Chavi?"

Moyra blew on the hot liquid. It smelled of peppermint. She took a sip, then said, "We need your help." She related the story, starting from when she was given the merlin by Lady Caroline's maid.

"Lady Caroline said her maid was a Traveler too. Do you know her?"

He shook his head. "I haven't been outside Curston's walls in years. Haven't followed *patrin*."

"What's that?" Driskoll asked.

"A secret language using grass and leaves," Moyra answered.

"A way we talk so *gorgio*—non-Travelers—do not know everything about us," Rom explained further. "I have not met any new Travelers through *patrin* in a long time."

Kellach pulled the silver key out of the pouch on his belt

and showed it to Rom. "We think the symbol on the key may be a clue, like a map, leading us to the crypt. Is it some kind of *patrin* too?"

The circle-and-ray markings on the key threw back the firelight in golden sparks, as if defying the kids to interpret their meaning.

After a pause, Rom reached out and took the key, which was nearly swallowed in his big fingers. He turned it over thoughtfully, then winced as if suddenly struck by pain. He tossed the key to the floor.

"What is it, Rom?" Moyra scooped up the key and tucked it in her pocket.

"You are right. It is a map," he replied softly. "But it is the other side of the key you should worry about."

"The griffon?" Kellach asked. "It's supposed to match the one on the crypt. That's all we know about it."

"There is more," Rom said. His cheerful demeanor darkened, like rain clouds blotting out the sun. "But the key can only be read by those who can see Beyond."

"So you *have* been to Deeping Well!" Driskoll cried. "I knew it!"

"You can see Beyond?" Kellach was impressed.

"Yes, but it is dangerous. I can only look a few seconds at a time or—" Rom shook his head.

Moyra tapped Rom on the knee. "You don't have to do this if you don't want to."

Rom's brows rushed together like thunderheads. "We do not have a choice, do we, Chavi? I would rather die than see Curston destroyed by a cowardly wizard who hides behind another man's grief." Rom gave a long sigh, then gestured toward the cupboard over the hearth. "There is parchment there, along with quill and ink. Fetch them, Chavi, please."

When Moyra returned with the items, Rom turned to Kellach. "I know you have learning. Write down what I say. I may not remember when I—come back."

Kellach pulled up a vacant stool to use as a makeshift desk. Then he dipped the turkey feather into the jar of pokeberry ink. "Ready."

Moyra handed Rom the key. He closed his eyes and stroked the griffon carved in the handle with his thumb. He rocked back and forth slowly, humming tunelessly. Then his lips parted and he spoke.

"Green . . ." he murmured, his voice distant. "Trees . . . roads . . . no, not roads . . . something between the trees . . . something *from* the trees . . ."

Kellach scribbled frantically.

Rom went on. His voice grew loud and agitated. "Circles . . . circ—something . . . *arrggghhh!*" His features twisted in agony. His fingers clutched the key in a death grip.

"Get that key away from him!" Moyra screamed. "It's hurting him!" She hurled herself across the rug and grabbed Rom's hand. "Help me!"

Kellach flung the quill away and sprang forward. He and Moyra wrestled to pry the big man's fingers open, but Rom's strength was tremendous.

"*Arrrgh! Arrgh!*" Rom's face turned purplish red as he clenched the key even tighter. He was clearly in the vise of a force that aimed to destroy him before it turned him loose.

"Kellach!" Moyra pulled Rom's fingers with all her might. "*Do* something!"

"Let go," Kellach told Moyra.

"What?"

"LET GO!"

She backed away.

Clasping Rom's fist in his two hands, Kellach muttered, "*Wooshter!*"

Instantly, Rom's fingers flew open. The key sailed halfway across the room and clattered to the floor.

Moyra snatched it up, fearing it would scorch her fingers. Amazingly, the carved silver was cool to the touch and lay innocently in the palm of her hand.

Rom opened his eyes and saw Kellach kneeling before him.

"I heard you," he said weakly. "I heard you say the Traveler word for 'throw.' Why did you use my language? Not even Chavi can speak it."

Kellach stood up. "That spell can only work in another

language besides Common. I figured the Traveler tongue would be best." He rubbed his back. "Whew! You're pretty strong!"

"Can you tell us what you saw?" Moyra asked, handing Rom his half-drunk mug of tea. "Kellach wrote everything down, but it didn't make much sense. Did you see the crypt?"

Rom took a long swallow of tea. "The *mulladipoov*—crypt—is outside Curston's walls. But not far."

"Is it in the forest?" Kellach asked, checking his parchment. "You mentioned green. And trees."

Rom nodded.

Moyra took in a slow breath. "That must be the Great Forest, right, Kellach?"

Driskoll glanced nervously from Moyra to his brother. "The Great Forest? But that's filled with all sorts of creepy creatures. Trolls and ogres and . . ." Driskoll didn't finish his thought.

Kellach took the key from Moyra and put it in one of the pouches he wore on his belt. "Like Rom said, we have no choice. If we have to go to the Great Forest, we will." He turned back to the Traveler. "Rom, you kept talking about circles. Are the circles in the woods?"

"Yes. They seemed to be roads, but I couldn't tell for sure." Suddenly Rom set his mug on the table with a clunk. "I saw something else," he whispered. "The *Juckal* lives there."

Moyra knew that word. "What dog?" she asked. "A dog lives in the forest?"

Rom passed a shaky hand before his eyes. "No, not a dog.

Something *like* a dog. Only much bigger. And white. White as snow. It comes from the woods."

Moyra's heart skipped. "The white blizzard thing that followed us from the No Name Pub!" She felt the tuft of long, white fur in her pocket and pulled it out. "I found this on my boot when somebody—or something—chased us earlier today."

Rom stared at the scrap of white fur. He made no move to touch it.

"You have seen the *Juckal*," he said hoarsely.

"Not exactly," Driskoll replied. "All we saw was a lot of white, like a snowstorm. What is a—what did you call it?"

"The *Juckal*. But that is not its true name," said Rom. "That is what it is called in *pattrimishis*—fairy tales."

"That thing that was after us is no fairy tale!" Driskoll said.

Kellach held up his hand. "We have enough to worry about at the moment. Let's concentrate on finding the crypt. Thanks for helping us, Rom."

"You three be careful," Rom said. "You will need *kushti bak*—good luck." He rummaged in the cupboard and lifted out a small wooden box. He opened the box and gave a brittle ivory stick to Driskoll. "This is for you."

"Thanks. Er—what is it?"

"Breastbone of a bird. A kingfisher's. Very powerful."

Next Rom gave Moyra a tiny vellum envelope. A dried bit of greenery could be seen inside.

"A four-leaf clover," Moyra said. "Thanks so much, Rom."

The last item was a knobbed pinkish rock. He gave that to Kellach. "This is a magic stone from the sea," he said. "It will protect you from evil spirits."

"Thanks," Kellach said. He added the coral to the pouch with the key. "And now we really must go."

Rom walked them to the door. He put his hand on Moyra's shoulder. "You," he said quietly, "have connected with the *Juckal*. It will seek you out. Be wary."

Moyra felt a shiver tiptoe down her spine.

Then Rom shut the door.

Outside, the sky over the Cathedral of St. Cuthbert's was tinted purple. When the sun went down, the watchers enforced curfew, and everyone had to be off the streets. Shady creatures that shunned the light of day crept out to prey on anyone foolish enough to be out after dark, especially in Broken Town.

"I guess that's it for today," Kellach said to Moyra. "Do you want us to walk you—"

Just then something swooshed down from the rooftops and flapped in their faces. Moyra put her hands over her head, but then she recognized the small cream-and-brown-colored bird. The merlin settled on her arm, blinking.

"Lady Caroline's bird!" Driskoll cried.

Kellach pointed to a tiny scroll tied to the bird's leg with copper thread. "Hold the bird, Moyra, while I untie it."

Moyra held her arm upright and still. "Nice bird. Don't bite me."

Kellach untied the thread, removed the tiny scroll, and unrolled it.

"It's from Lady Caroline!" he said. "She wants us to come to Dardley Hall. She says it's urgent."

"Tomorrow, I hope," said Driskoll. "My feet are dying for a rest."

Moyra read the note over Kellach's shoulder. "Tell your feet to wake up. We have to meet Lady Caroline. *After* curfew."

CHAPTER

7

Moyra hurried through the Phoenix Quarter, headed for the Oldgate. Fog billowed down the streets. It felt like walking through ghosts.

Wasn't that what Kellach had said at the No Name Pub? Now she knew what he meant. A little chilly, a little mysterious, and very, very creepy.

Anyone—and any*thing*—could be out here.

She reached the city wall without any watchers spotting her, and huddled against the cold stone hidden by the shadows. She glanced up and down the street. They had agreed to meet there an hour after curfew. *She* was on time. Where were Kellach and Driskoll?

The face of a young half-orc leered at her, showing small, pointed teeth.

"A nice li'l girl," he said smugly. "An' I was jus' lookin' for a morsel—"

Moyra whipped out her dagger and thrust it inches from the creature's hairy nose.

"Go back in the sewer you crawled out of before I count to three. One—"

The half-orc scurried away, his long arms trailing behind him.

Moments later, Moyra heard the patter of hurrying feet. Once more, her hand flew to her dagger hilt.

Kellach and Driskoll materialized before her. Shreds of fog clung to them. They looked like ghosts themselves. Moyra relaxed.

"Should have known you'd be late," she said.

"It's Dad's night off," Kellach explained. "We had to wait until he went to bed."

"Then we had to sneak out the window," added Driskoll. "Did you have trouble leaving your house?"

"Of course not."

"Sometimes I think you can slip through keyholes," said Driskoll.

"When it comes to getting in and out of places, Moyra isn't bound by the same laws as ordinary people," Kellach said.

Moyra grinned.

Kellach pointed to the towering, ironbound gate. Two huge watchers stood before it. "So how are you planning to get through that? They won't open the gate for anyone."

Moyra kicked at a small stone at the base of the city wall

behind her. "So we won't go through the gate."

With a few more swift kicks, the stone popped free. Moyra heaved it aside, revealing a hole in the wall about the size of a trapdoor. "My dad showed me this spot. Of course he's a bit too fat to squeeze through here, but it's just right for kids." She glanced over her shoulder to make sure the watchers hadn't seen them, then gestured through the dark hole. "After you, boys."

Driskoll and Kellach dropped down on their stomachs and slid through the hole. After Moyra had poked through, she pulled the stone back into place and they headed down the road toward Dardley Hall.

█ █ █ █ █

About thirty minutes later, Moyra and the two boys stood outside Dardley Hall's private wall with its forbidding gates. Moyra peered through the iron bars of the gate.

The crowds of the Mop Fair were long gone, and the enormous manor house towered above the courtyard. If Dardley Manor had been built in Broken Town, Moyra thought, it would take up at least two blocks. The massive front door looked as big as her family's house.

"See that?" Kellach pointed to the bowed windows jutting from the front of the manor. "That's Lord Dardley's private chambers."

Warm yellow light poured from the high arched windows.

Figures flitted back and forth. While it was muffled and ghostly outside, activity bustled inside.

"What do we do now?" Driskoll asked. "All Lady Caroline said was to meet her here after curfew."

"She'll be here," Kellach said. He tugged on the iron bars. "Locked. Lord Dardley's private guards are undoubtedly stationed on the battlements."

Moyra eyed the latch. "Want me to pick the lock? I brought my equipment."

"Let's wait a little longer," Kellach told her.

"How long?" Moyra hated waiting for anything. "It's cold and miserable out here. I'm not thrilled about—"

Just then a pale hand reached out of the fog and tapped Moyra on the shoulder.

She jumped.

A figure in a silver-gray cape stepped out of the mist. "Shh! It's me!"

"Lady Caroline!" Moyra whispered hoarsely. "You scared me half to death!"

"I'm sorry I'm late. I had to come the back way to meet you here. Follow me. Stay close to the wall." With a whirl of silver-gray velvet, Lady Caroline disappeared into the fog again.

The kids walked in a tight bunch. Every so often, Lady Caroline would look back to make sure they were still behind her. As they rounded the back of the wall, she put out her hand, motioning for them to stop.

She pointed up at a rope dangling over the high stone wall. "We'll have to climb. Meet me on the other side."

Without another word, she flung back the hood of her cape. Her golden hair twisted down her back in a loose braid. Grasping the rope with both hands, she walked up the wall. At the top, she turned around, pulled the rope after her, then disappeared.

Moyra was impressed. She thought ladies of the manor were delicate creatures. Lady Caroline was definitely not fragile.

The rope snaked back over their side of the wall.

"Dris, you go next," Kellach said. "And don't take all night."

"I'm no slower than you are," Driskoll said defensively. He leaped at the rope, trying to jump halfway up the wall. For his trouble, he received a nasty rope burn. He struggled the rest of the way up.

Kellach and Moyra watched until Driskoll was out of sight. The rope flapped over their side of the wall again.

"My turn." Moyra tugged on the dangling rope to make sure it was secure, then scrambled up. At the top, she tossed the rope down to Kellach.

He tied a loop at the end of the rope, put his foot in the loop and muttered something under his breath. The rope stiffened and he sailed up and over the wall. He dropped inside the fog-shrouded courtyard.

"You cheated," Moyra said, scrambling down the other side.

"It's not cheating to use my skills." Kellach made another

gesture in the air. The rope dropped in a neat coil on the ground.

"Clever," Lady Caroline remarked. "Now, we must make haste. We haven't much time." She ran lightly across the grass, with her cloak fluttering behind her.

"Why can't she for *once* tell us what we are going to do next?" Driskoll muttered as he rushed to keep up.

Lady Caroline guided them toward the back of the manor, into deep shadows. Moyra was amazed to see a number of wooden outbuildings behind the manor. She recognized a smithy, a smokehouse, a cooper's and a wheelwright's sheds, and a stable large enough to house teams of horses. It was like a small village, all to support Dardley Hall.

"Aren't we going in the house?" Kellach asked.

"My father is in his private office, where Nimrae is attending to his every need," Lady Caroline replied, her tone acid with sarcasm. "But they might come out, and I don't want Nimrae to see you. He'll know I've asked you to help me fight against him. Anyway, what I want you to see isn't in the house."

They followed Lady Caroline to the stables. Beside the stables was a small thatched building. As they approached, squawks and caws issued from within.

"What's that?" Driskoll asked fearfully.

"The mews," replied Lady Caroline. "Where our hunting birds—our hawks and falcons—are kept. They'll be quiet once we're inside."

"Inside?" Moyra asked. She stopped walking. "What exactly is it that you want us to do?"

Lady Caroline looked over her shoulder and then whispered, "When I returned home after our meeting this afternoon, my father mentioned there had been a mysterious prowler in the stables."

"Did he see the prowler?" Kellach asked.

"No. Wat, one of our servants, mentioned it. He claimed something was bothering the animals. But he was too frightened to investigate for himself. I need you to hide in the stables in case this prowler returns."

Moyra rolled her eyes. "Why don't you get one of your guards to do this? Why us?"

Lady Caroline grasped Moyra's shoulders. "You're the only ones I can trust." She looked around. "I suspect this prowler may be one of Nimrae's spies. Perhaps if you can find out who he is and what he wants, we'll be able to stop this whole business before it even begins."

A shiver ran up Moyra's spine. She wasn't afraid as much as she was overcome by an ominous feeling. The prowler, she thought, is here. Watching us.

Lady Caroline rapped on the stable door. After a few seconds, they could hear a bar being lifted, then one of the double doors swung inward.

A short, crooked figure stood silhouetted in the doorway holding a half-shuttered lantern.

"Come in, m'lady," he said, ushering them all inside. "Make quick, before the guard makes his rounds."

Moyra breathed in the earthy smell of animals, hay, and manure. She heard the gentle movements of horses stirring in their stalls. A small fire burned in a grate-topped pot in the middle of the floor. Its warmth melted the bone-chilling dampness.

Three bloodhounds leaped at Moyra's feet, but they were quickly calmed by a swift hand signal from the person who had let them in.

The figure opened the lantern. In full light, Moyra could see he was a boy no older than Driskoll. Unruly hair fanned over wide-set blue eyes. The boy wore an ugly boot with a thick wooden sole and walked with a limp.

"Wat," said Lady Caroline. "This is Kellach, Driskoll, and Moyra. They are here to help catch the prowler. We can trust them."

"Yes, m'lady." Wat tugged his forelock.

"Have you seen the prowler this evening?" Kellach asked.

"Not yet." Wat cut his eyes toward the door.

Lady Caroline looked at Kellach. "Can you all spend the night here? It's important."

"I suppose," Kellach said. "As long as we return by dawn."

"Thank you." She drew the hood of her cloak over her head. "Be careful."

Wat unlatched the door for her, and she disappeared into the night, her gray cape blending into the fog.

Driskoll yawned. "Where are our beds?"

Moyra snorted. "We're not here to sleep, Dris! We're supposed to be waiting to catch a prowler."

Driskoll shrugged. "But I'm so sleepy, I can't stand up another second."

"Here." Wat pointed to a scattering of straw the dogs were nestled in.

"With the *dogs*? I said I'm tired, not desperate."

"Dogs warm." Wat leaned against the solid body of the bloodhound. The dog snuffled and made room for the boy.

"We might as well make ourselves comfortable while we wait." Kellach knelt on the floor, gathering straw to form a sort of mattress. "The dogs are friendly, aren't they?"

"Dogs friendly." Wat cuddled against the bloodhound, then looked back at Kellach. "To some people."

Driskoll didn't seem reassured, but he followed Kellach's lead and scraped a bit of hay together at the edge of the dogs' nest.

"Oh, for Cuthbert's sake," Moyra said. She flopped down next to the bloodhound. "What's your name, boy?" The dog licked her nose in reply.

Wat leaned over and extinguished the lantern.

Darkness dropped as if a giant tapestry tented the estate.

No moon shone, or if it did, the light couldn't penetrate the dense fog.

Moyra tried to find a comfortable position on the hard floor. It was so black inside the stable that she lost all sense of orientation. She couldn't tell whether her eyes were open or closed. Growing up in the chaos of Broken Town, she wasn't easily frightened. But she was unable to relax in this strange place.

She lay there for what seemed like hours.

She could hear Driskoll softly snoring. The dogs twitched and whimpered in their sleep. The horses shifted their feet. Moyra heard soft breathing, in, out, in, out . . . Was that the horses too?

Then her sharp ears picked up another sound. She tensed. It was the drawn-out *skreek* of a door being eased open. She heard something breathing heavily. Then footfalls padded across the floor.

Closer.

Closer.

"Kell—" she gasped, but someone clamped a hand over her mouth.

The sound of the prowler's breathing grew louder and louder and closer and closer until she thought she could feel its heat on her skin.

Wat struck a tinder. The lantern flared to life again.

Into the circle of light padded an enormous white wolf.

Its body was the size of a draft horse, its eyes bigger than pewter plates. The wolf opened its mouth, revealing dozens of gleaming fangs.

Moyra's heart stopped.

The *Juckal*.

CHAPTER

8

A iiieee!" Wat dropped the lantern and bolted for the door, flying past the beast with amazing speed despite his limp.

The door stood wide open, but Wat didn't stop to question how the inside bar had been removed. He tore outside, flinging screams behind him in the chilly air.

The hand covering Moyra's mouth went limp, and she turned to see Kellach beside her—his body stiff with fear. She didn't blame him. The creature was so big that it could be measured in hands, like one of the stabled horses.

The wolf stared at Moyra. She felt him capture her gaze. Rom's warning had come true. The wolf had sought her out. But why? What did he want from her?

"Fire!" Driskoll cried. "The lantern!"

Moyra whirled around. Tiny flames leaped from the fallen lantern and licked at the straw. Shadows leaped on the far wall, and the smell of smoke filled Moyra's nostrils.

Jerked out of his trance, Kellach began beating at knee-high flames with his cloak. Driskoll stood beside him, stamping the flames with his boots.

The three dogs sprang up, trembling and whining. They milled around in a restless circle, unable to decide which was the greatest danger—the fire or the enormous wolf. In their stalls, the horses kicked and whinnied nervously.

Kellach and Driskoll kept fighting the fire. But the flames refused to die.

"Moyra!" Driskoll cried. "We need water!"

Moyra raced to the feed bin. She found a big bucket full of water beside it and sloshed it on the center of the fire. The flames shot toward the beams overhead, then died down.

Moyra took in a deep breath and surveyed the damage.

Kellach's cloak was ruined. Black ashes streaked his cheeks. Driskoll's boots were black with soot. Moyra's face felt scorched.

She closed her eyes, praying the commotion had scared away the giant beast poised to attack them. She turned.

The wolf was still there.

He hadn't moved an inch. His eyes were a pale blue, nearly as white as his coat, and seemed to have no pupils. He stood there, simply watching her.

Then, after a moment, he placed a ham-sized paw on the singed straw and stepped closer, slowly and deliberately. His back muscles rippled with the motion. One spring and he would have any of them between his powerful, traplike jaws.

The bloodhounds whimpered. Moyra might have whimpered herself if she had any spit left. Her mouth was as dry as the charred straw beneath her boots.

"Um, Kell?" Driskoll asked his brother out of the side of his mouth. "Do you think you should *do* something?"

Kellach clenched his fists. "I'm thinking," he whispered.

"Can't you make him disappear or something?" Moyra asked.

"He's too big."

The wolf's big blue eyes focused intently on Kellach.

"I think he understands what you are saying," Moyra said.

Kellach's eyes went wide. "He does!"

Driskoll wrinkled his nose. "You can hear him?"

Kellach shook his head. "He's speaking to me through my mind. Like the asperis did when we were up in the mountains. But I think he can only speak to a wizard, like me." Kellach smiled a self-satisfied grin. "It's amazing. His words feel soft and smooth like—like water gliding over rocks in a creek."

Moyra crossed her arms. "I don't care what it feels like. What's he saying?"

Kellach held up his hand and leaned closer toward the wolf. "I'm—I'm Kellach," he said aloud. He turned back to Moyra. "His name is Moonshadow."

"Great." Moyra smirked. "It's always good to know the name of the beast before it eats you."

Kellach glared at her. "He says he's friendly." Kellach turned back to the wolf. "What do you want from us? Why are you here?" He paused for a moment, then he relayed Moonshadow's answer. "He says he's here to help the Seekers."

Driskoll frowned. "Seekers? What Seekers? Are they Nimrae's spies?"

Kellach listened for a moment, then explained. "*We're* the Seekers. Those who seek the tomb of the dead Knights."

"How does he know we are looking for the crypt?" Moyra asked.

"He says his master told him," Kellach replied.

"Master? Is he a familiar?" Moyra was still suspicious. "I'm not sure I trust a talking wolf, even one that claims to be friendly. How do we know he isn't sizing us up for a late supper?"

"Shhh!" Driskoll said. "Kellach, ask him why he came here."

"He says his master sent him to find us. He tried to talk to us earlier today, but we ran into the bad-smelling den—"

"The warehouse." Moyra nodded. "Then how did he know to come *here*?"

Kellach paused. "Moonshadow says he picked up our scent on the grounds earlier today. He knew that sooner or later we'd come back. Who is your master?" Kellach asked the wolf.

Moonshadow turned to leave.

"Wait!" Kellach cried, holding out his arms as if to pull

the wolf back. "Who is your master? And the crypt! Can you help us find it?"

Moonshadow nodded his massive white head.

"How? Where is it?" Moyra asked.

Kellach's arms dropped to his sides. "All he will say is that he was sent to tell us his master can help us. He says that tomorrow we will learn more."

"Tomorrow!" Driskoll stomped his foot. "We only have three days left!"

But the wolf did not answer. As silently as he came into the stables, he loped away through the double doors. A gust of wind from the outside blasted in, scattering wisps of singed straw.

Moyra stared after the wolf. "Do you think he's one of Nimrae's spies?"

Kellach swiped a sooty hand across his chin. "No way. Moonshadow entered my mind as easily as you open locks, Moyra. I believe him when he says he's friendly. I wasn't worried when I was talking to him."

"*We* were," Driskoll said. "Do you think he files those great big fangs to punch out paper hearts?"

Kellach scowled. "We have to start looking for the crypt somewhere. That wolf may be the answer to our prayers."

"But he doesn't know where the crypt is," Driskoll said. "Maybe not, but he knows someone who may," Kellach fired back. "And that someone will be in touch with us."

"Soon, I hope," Moyra said. "Can we go home now? I'm dead on my feet."

Driskoll shivered. "Don't say that word."

The kids left, closing the doors to the stable. They looked around the grounds for a moment, but Wat was nowhere to be found. Moyra hoped the stableboy wouldn't get in trouble for abandoning his post and causing what could have been a devastating fire.

She wrapped her thin jacket around her and yawned as they skulked along the wall, looking for the climbing rope. Idly she wondered how Moonshadow gained entrance into the estate. But right now she was too tired to think. All she wanted was home and her bed.

CHAPTER

9

The next morning, Moyra woke with a start. It wasn't daylight yet, but she heard her father's voice. She hadn't seen her father for a few days, and when Breddo was home, he usually slept till noon.

Something must be up.

Hopping out of bed, she quickly dressed, burying her smoky clothes from the night before under the basket of washing. Then she hurried into the kitchen.

Her mother was setting a plate of fried eggs in front of her father. Eggs! Usually they had bread sopped in grease for breakfast. Did her father buy eggs? Or steal them?

"There's my slugabed," Breddo teased. "Have you heard my news?"

Moyra sat down across from him at the table. "What news, Daddy?"

"I'm going on a big hunt today."

"You're what?" She rubbed her ear and wondered if she were still asleep. Her father didn't go hunting, unless he was poaching.

Royma grinned broadly as she set a plate of eggs in front of Moyra. "You heard him, girl. Your father's gotten a decent job for the first time in his life. I'm so proud." Royma planted a quick kiss on Breddo's clean-shaven face and sat down beside him. "He got hired yesterday at the Mop Fair."

"A-yup," Breddo said. "I went to the Mop Fair to pick some pockets, but uh . . . I didn't have much luck."

Moyra grimaced. Her father was one of the worst pick-pockets in Curston. He had probably been nearly caught picking some nobleman's pocket and decided to give up while he was ahead. Even though Moyra didn't look down on thieves—after all, she was one herself—she wished that her father could find a profession that he was at least *good* at doing.

"So I thought"—Breddo tilted his chair on two legs—"why not look for a real job, like your old mom is always saying. I offered myself up as a beater, and one of Lord Dardley's swells hired me on the spot."

Moyra took a bite of egg. "What's a beater?"

He laughed heartily. "I beat the bushes to drive out game. Copper-a-day wages."

Royma's eyes shone. "I might not have to work so hard at the market with that money coming in. And your father won't need to do any more thieving."

Breddo rubbed Royma's hand. "I wasn't expecting to start work yet, but one of Dardley's messengers came by this morning to tell me a hunt was on for today. He said today's just a trial, but if I can manage to help Dardley's men catch the wolf they're after, I may be hired on as a huntsman at Dardley Hall full time!"

Moyra had never seen her parents so happy. She didn't need a charm to fix their problems after all. Warmth filled her heart. "That's wonderful, Daddy."

Then a terrible thought clouded her happiness. If she and Kellach and Driskoll didn't find the crypt and raise the Knights to fight Nimrae's army, her father wouldn't need this fine job: Breddo—and everyone else in Curston—would be gone.

"What's the matter, baby?" Breddo patted Moyra's hand. "Don't you like the idea of me helping hunt a wolf?"

It wasn't until then that Breddo's words sunk in. Moyra stared at her father. "Did you say wolf?"

Breddo nodded as he mopped the last bit of eggs off his plate with a thick slice of bread.

Moyra remembered the white wolf they'd seen the night before. Moonshadow. Lord Dardley must be after him! But . . . if Lord Dardley was planning to hunt down the big wolf, it must mean Kellach was right. Moonshadow wasn't one of Nimrae's spies. He was their only hope of finding the crypt and saving Curston. She had to do something.

Moyra shot up out of her chair. "Dad! Can I go with you on

the hunt this morning? I'd love to . . . to see you in action."

"Well, you'll have to stay out of the way, but I don't see why not." Breddo looked to Royma. Royma picked up their plates, giving a small shrug.

"Thanks! I'll just get my jacket." Moyra raced into her room.

There was no time to lose. She had to warn Moonshadow. Before it was too late.

◦ ◦ ◦ ◦ ◦

The courtyard of Dardley Hall was a beehive of activity. The iron gates, locked so firmly the night before, stood wide open. Hunting dogs barked and strained at their handlers' leashes. Horses wore the Dardley Hall colors of scarlet and gold. Servants carried baskets and kegs to horses wearing special yokes.

A man in a scarlet and gold tunic stood in the center of the courtyard surrounded by several men from Broken Town.

"That's my boss over there," Breddo said as they crossed the gates. He leaned down and gave Moyra a quick hug. "I had better leave you here."

"Be careful, Dad."

She hurried back out the main gates. She wasn't sure how she was going to find Moonshadow, but she thought she might start by retracing their steps from the night before.

As she turned the corner, she bumped into Kellach and Driskoll.

"What in the Abyss are you two doing here?" she asked.

"We might ask the same," said Kellach.

"When I got up this morning, I found out that Dad's been hired as a beater on today's hunt." Moyra looked back over her shoulder before adding, "On today's *wolf* hunt!"

Kellach nodded. "We know all about the wolf hunt. We heard it from our dad. We came to warn Moonshadow."

Moyra heaved a sigh. "Me too."

Driskoll looked up at his brother. "I still don't understand why we need to protect Moonshadow."

Kellach rolled his eyes. "Don't you get it? He's our only hope of finding the crypt. If he's killed, then we'll never find it!"

"How are we going to find him?" Driskoll asked.

"I have a plan," Kellach said. "Just follow me."

Kellach led Driskoll and Moyra back to the courtyard. No one noticed three kids slip through the iron gates and duck behind the hedge lining the wall.

"Look!" Driskoll said, peeking through the branches. "There's Lady Caroline."

The young woman swept out the doors of the manor house wearing a scarlet riding gown. Her unbound hair streamed down her back. A gold circlet kept loose waves out of her eyes. Her left hand was covered with a padded leather glove.

Wat led a gray mare with a black mane and tail into the courtyard. The horse was outfitted with a lady's saddle and a gold-trimmed saddle blanket. Wat helped Lady Dardley mount so that she sat sidesaddle on her mare. The wide skirt of her gown fell over the mare's rump in graceful folds.

"Wat must not be in trouble," said Kellach. "I wonder if he told her what happened?"

"He must have told Lord Dardley at least," Moyra said. "Otherwise, how would they know to go on a wolf hunt?"

"Who are those two people with all the birds?" Driskoll asked.

They watched as a tall man and a boy brought out a ladder-like table and set it on the grass. Three hooded birds were tied by one leg to the perches along the table.

"That must be the falconer," Kellach said. "And his assistant."

The man untied a small bird, removed its hood, and gave it to Lady Caroline.

"That's Lady Caroline's merlin." Moyra felt a special bond with the bird.

The falconer then unhooded a bird Kellach said was a peregrine falcon, and he marched over to a dark-haired man striding toward a chestnut horse. The man wore polished high boots and a splendid scarlet tunic embroidered with gold thread. A curved hunting horn was strapped to his wrist.

"Lord Dardley," Kellach said.

"He doesn't look bewitched to me," Moyra whispered. If anything, the man looked giddy, as if he were having the time of his life.

The hunting party began to organize. Lord Dardley mounted the chestnut horse. The falconer handed him the peregrine falcon.

A man in black velvet robes came rushing down the manor steps. A mustache and beard, braided and decorated with small beads, flowed from beneath his hooked nose. His head was completely bald, but his bushy eyebrows formed a sinister *V* above his black eyes. A stableboy placed a stool next to a midnight black horse, and the man mounted the steed. The falconer's assistant unhooded the last bird perched on the table. It was a large gray hawk. He handed it to the man.

Kellach poked Moyra's arm. "That's the goshawk! Nimrae's familiar. Which means—"

"That man is Nimrae," Moyra finished. She memorized every detail of the house wizard, from his elaborate black beard to the heavy gold chains hanging from his robes.

Two huntsmen—one in a blue tunic, the other in green—fell in behind Lord Dardley, each carrying lances. The dog handlers wrestled with the eager pack of bloodhounds. Three servants stood behind the hunt cart, which was decorated with scarlet and gold streamers.

Beyond the cart, Moyra caught sight of a group of merchant Travelers unpacking a wagon. Soon the courtyard would be filled with tents from which all sorts of wares would be sold.

"It's like the Mop Fair all over again," Driskoll said.

"A hunt day *is* always a special occasion," Kellach said. "But

Lord Dardley doesn't usually have a hunt so soon after the Mop Fair. He must really want to find Moonshadow."

"Where's your dad, Moyra?" asked Driskoll.

She strained to see through the jostling parade. "There!"

Breddo strutted among the other beaters. He did a little dance, making all the Broken Town peasants laugh.

Moyra's heart sank. Why couldn't her father act like everyone else, instead of capering and fooling around like a jester?

"Look!" Kellach whispered. "They're moving."

But instead of heading toward the gates, the party filed around the manor house to the back. The kids followed, keeping a veil of shrubbery between them and the party.

"So what exactly is this brilliant plan of yours, Mr. Wizard?" Moyra whispered.

Kellach shrugged. "We'll follow the hunting party, and if they catch sight of Moonshadow, I'll create a diversion. Then you two can rush ahead and warn him."

"But what about—"

"Shhh!" Driskoll put a warning finger to his lips and pointed at the wall.

The hunting party pulled up at an arched wooden door set in the stone wall. Two guards opened it, and the hunters filed through one by one.

Kellach crouch-walked along the wall toward the door. "Look like we belong so the guards won't stop us."

They managed to slink out of their hiding place and blend with the tagalongs at the end of the hunting party. When the group halted on a wide path just inside the forest, the kids slipped into a hollow among the roots of a giant oak.

"How can Lord Dardley hunt in the woods outside of Curston? He doesn't own them," Moyra asked, glancing around the little hollow to make sure a fox or bear didn't attack them. She felt more comfortable in Broken Town than in the wilds of the forest.

"He owns part of it," Kellach answered. "I've heard my dad speak of Lord Dardley's private game preserve. The Great Forest beyond, though, is not part of his territory."

"How far does his land go?" Driskoll asked. "How does he know he's not in the Great Forest?"

"Maybe there's a wall," Kellach guessed. "I'm sure he doesn't want to wander off in the Great Forest."

Moyra shivered. She knew from personal experience that the forest crawled with giants, athachs, trolls, and all manner of frightening creatures.

Just then three rallying blasts sounded on Lord Dardley's hunting horn. The hunt had officially begun. From their leafy hiding place, the kids watched the huntsmen set off with the braying bloodhounds. The horses cantered behind them.

"They're heading out! Quick!" But as Moyra crawled out from their hiding place, she saw Lady Caroline wheel her mare, her merlin flapping on her upraised fist.

Moyra gasped, and Driskoll pulled her back into the hollow by her ankles.

Lady Caroline stared hard at the giant oak tree as if she could see them. With a slight nod, she reined her horse back around and galloped to join the party.

"She knows we're here," Driskoll said. "How?"

"I don't know," said Moyra. "Why hasn't she contacted us? Wasn't she worried about us after last night?"

"Maybe that look she just gave us is her way of saying she'll be in touch," Kellach said. "She probably wants us to let the party get far enough ahead so they won't see us."

The three kids waited in silence. Birds called from the treetops. Small creatures rustled in the underbrush. It was not unheard of to be whisked away by tree spirits. Moyra was trying to remember the warning smell a dryad gave off when Kellach gave a nod. "I think it's safe now."

They climbed out of the hollow and walked down the path. The party was so far ahead that they heard no ringing voices and no stamping of horses' hooves. The path forked.

"They went this way," said Kellach, heading left.

"Are you sure?" asked Moyra. "I think it's this way." She pointed to the fork on the right.

"No, left. See? This path is dusty from the cart and horses," Kellach insisted.

After they had walked for what seemed likc forever without a glimpse of the hunting party, Kellach paused.

Moyra crossed her arms. "You're lost."

Kellach stared down at the ground. "I'm not lost . . . I'm searching for tracks. I'm sure I'll find them again."

"Right." Moyra rolled her eyes. "I knew we should have taken the right fork."

Moyra squinted up at the sun to gauge the time. But dark gray clouds blanketed the sky, completely obscuring the morning sun. She had no idea how long they'd been out here. For all she knew, the hunt could be over, and Moonshadow could be . . .

Moyra gulped and glanced back at Kellach. "Hurry up! We've got to keep moving. Pick a direction!"

"We're definitely lost." Driskoll flopped down to the ground and put his chin in his hands.

"We're not lost," Kellach said stubbornly. "Just give me a minute—"

Moyra fixed him with a no-nonsense stare. "We are lost! Why don't you just admit it and let us help?"

Help . . . help. . . help . . .

The echo skipped around them, as if a dozen taunting goblins were posted behind the trees ready to spring at any second. The trees themselves seemed to be closer than they had been before, as if they had crept forward when the kids weren't watching.

"Fine!" Kellach threw up his arms. "We're lost."

"Now what?" Driskoll asked. "Can't you summon a horse or something to get us out of here?"

"Sure, but a horse won't do us any good if we don't know where we want it to take us. Horses need direction."

The bushes rustled. Not from a small scurrying creature, but from something much bigger moving deliberately in their direction.

"Something's coming!" Moyra pulled her dagger from its sheath.

Driskoll leaped to his feet, his hand on his sword hilt. Kellach held up both hands, warning them not to take any action yet, not until they actually saw the enemy.

The crashing sound grew louder.

"How *big* is this thing?" Driskoll muttered, trying to sound brave. He gripped his sword tighter. The tension in the clearing grew thicker. Moyra's mouth became as dry as untanned leather.

A gigantic white furry face parted the bushes.

"Moonshadow!" Moyra's legs went weak with relief. "We were worried about—"

She stopped.

The wolf was not alone.

CHAPTER

10

An elderly man walked behind Moonshadow, gripping a braided grapevine as a leash in one wrinkled hand. The man wore a tattered blue woolen cloak that hooded his face, and crudely stitched slippers. His tunic hung loosely from scarecrow shoulders, down to his bony knees. He was so thin that a brisk wind could blow him over.

"Can we help you, sir?" Kellach asked.

"I understand that you are the ones in need of help." The old man looked just beyond Kellach's left ear.

Kellach turned around but saw nothing.

The man threw back his hood, revealing long white scraggly hair that almost hid the hideous scars around his milky blue eyes.

Moyra elbowed Kellach and whispered, "He's blind! Moonshadow's leading him on that leash."

Moyra turned back to face the man. "You're the master

Moonshadow told us about last night, aren't you?"

The old man nodded. "Moonshadow heard your cry for help and brought me here." He patted Moonshadow's massive head as if the wolf were a lady's lapdog.

"We actually came here to help Moonshadow," Driskoll said. "We believe Lord Dardley is after him. He's on a wolf hunt in these woods."

"But we lost the hunting party a while back." Moyra looked pointedly at Kellach. "We're not sure where we are."

"Not sure where you are!" The old man's voice was scratchy, as if he weren't used to speaking. "You are the Seekers, are you not? You seek the tomb of the dead Knights?"

"How do you know we are the Seekers?" Moyra asked.

"My eyes—or what is left of them—ache a few days before the anniversary," the old man rasped. "But this year, I feel no pain. I sensed someone was seeking the crypt. I sent Moonshadow to find you."

"Who are you?" Kellach asked.

The man took a step back and swept into a deep bow. "I apologize for my lack of manners. I haven't properly introduced myself. I am Alaric. Rather, I used to be *Sir* Alaric, Knight of the Silver Dragon."

"You're a Knight of the Silver Dragon?" Driskoll stared at the old man and slowly backed away. "But we thought—"

"That we're all dead?" Alaric smiled. "Have no fear, lad. I'm not a ghost. Just a sorry excuse for a Knight."

"But how can you be a Knight of the Silver Dragon?" Kellach stared at the frail old man suspiciously. "We're Knights of the Silver Dragon. The day we joined the order, Zendric told us we were the only living Knights remaining besides him."

"Zendric speaks the truth." Alaric hung his head.

Kellach knitted his brow. "But . . . I don't understand."

Alaric sighed. "Let's sit, shall we? I have a long story to tell."

The kids sat on a log. Moonshadow lay down, and Alaric perched on his back as if the wolf were a cushioned bench. Moyra guessed the skinny man didn't weigh any more than a guinea hen.

"Zendric does not know I'm alive," Alaric said in his raspy voice. "I was supposed to be dead, like the others. Killed in the Troll Invasion."

"The Troll Invasion?" Kellach echoed. "You mean the battle where Lord Dardley lost his life?"

Alaric nodded.

"Then you must know Zendric didn't murder Lord Dardley," Kellach pressed. "I'm right, aren't I?"

"Yes. The great wizard did not lay a wand on Sir Dardley. He was nowhere near the battle that day."

"Why don't you come forward to the present Lord Dardley and tell him?" Moyra said. "We'll take you to his daughter, Lady Caroline."

A pained expression crossed Alaric's features. Moonshadow

whimpered in sympathy. Moyra wondered if the elderly knight was ill.

Alaric rubbed knobby knuckles over his eyes. "I wish I could. But it's not that simple."

"But if you were there—" Driskoll began.

Alaric held up one frail hand. "Let me begin at the beginning, child." He cleared his throat and, somehow, his voice sounded stronger. "You see, in my day, the Order of the Knights of the Silver Dragon was filled with the bravest and wisest men and women of Curston. We weren't just warriors—no, we were wizards and rogues, clerics and bards. And even though the first Lord Dardley wasn't a full-fledged resident of Curston, we counted him as one of our own. So when Dardley told us trolls were planning an invasion of Dardley Hall, a small group of us Knights—ten of his closest comrades—vowed to protect his land.

"We fought in the early morning," Alaric continued. "Mists had not yet dissipated over the fields. No one had a sign the fight would be different from any other battles with the mace-wielding brutes. We formed ranks and faced our enemy. Dardley's own guards formed the first line of battle. They carried eighteen-foot-long pikes that were certain to keep the enemy at bay. The trolls stomped the ground in eager anticipation and swung their flails."

Moyra's mind was already drawing mental pictures of the battle scene. She leaned forward, hanging on the old Knight's every word.

Alaric continued. "My fellow Knights and I lined up behind Dardley's guards. I had brought my horse, Ajax, to the battle. Dardley had warned me not to, but Ajax was a battle-seasoned steed. I trusted him to carry me into the fight, and out, unhurt, as he had a dozen previous battles. Like the enemy, Ajax stamped his feet, waiting for the fight to begin." Alaric's voice dropped to a whisper. "When he did, the world came to an end."

"How?" Kellach asked.

Alaric shook his head. "I'm getting ahead of myself. First the guards charged with their pikes pointed at the trolls' chests. They should have mowed down at least the first rank of trolls. But Dardley's guards were tossed aside like children's playthings. The trolls heaved their maces and flails to and fro. More guards died.

"Ajax galloped to the front, heading into another wave of charging trolls. Then Dardley gave the signal. You see, he had a secret weapon. Not a mechanical device, like a catapult. Not a battering ram or boiling oil. It was something neither the trolls nor I could ever have imagined . . . "

"What was it?" Driskoll breathed.

"Its head and upper body were that of a giant eagle. Great wings beat the air. The rest of its body belonged to a lion."

Kellach gave a low whistle. "A griffon."

Alaric nodded. "It was Dardley's. It was meant to charge the trolls. To lay waste to them. But he had trained the griffon in haste. And something went terribly wrong. Instead of charging

85

the trolls, the griffon went berserk. Griffons are the mortal enemies of horses, you know. They cannot resist the temptation of a horse's flesh. I knew then why Dardley had warned me not to bring Ajax. But it was too late.

"Ajax was terrified. He couldn't help but rear, unseating me. I fell underneath my horse. Ajax struggled to rise. I rolled out of the way, but my visor had flipped up. The griffon clawed my eyes. Ajax attacked, but . . . my brave horse lost the fight." Alaric's voice cracked, and he swallowed hard.

Moyra placed a hand on his arm. "Are you all right?"

The old man nodded. "I'm sorry. It's difficult to remember the details after all these years . . ." Alaric gulped. "As you might imagine, I was blinded. I crawled around on all fours, trying to reach safety. I heard Dardley rushing into the clearing to help me. I heard the swinging of a troll's mace. 'Alaric, help me!' Dardley begged. But how could I help? Next I heard a scuffle, Dardley's cries, and then silence. He was dead." Alaric's voice cracked again. "I failed my fellow Knight . . . I failed my friend."

"But you couldn't see," Driskoll said.

"I could have done something." The Knight shook his head. "I broke the code and for that I had to punish myself. I renounced my membership in the Order of the Knights of the Silver Dragon. From then on, I wandered the forest sightless, homeless, and helpless. If I hadn't met Moonshadow, I would have starved or frozen to death. My fellow Knights believed I had died in battle. And I let them believe it."

"I don't understand—the griffon was supposed to be Lord Dardley's ally," Moyra said. "But it hurt you instead. How could it do that? Wasn't it supposed to be fighting for the good?"

"Griffons are fair-weather allies, my child. They are neither good nor evil. They only live for themselves. Some can be trained to work for justice. Some cannot. This one . . . could not."

"What happened after the battle?" Kellach asked. "Did the trolls take over the land?"

"Dardley's guards were eventually victorious. But when Dardley's son returned home, he was furious that the Knights of the Silver Dragon, the order his father had so long served, had failed to save his father. Rather than returning the bodies of the fallen Knights to their families, he insisted that all the Knights be buried in a secret tomb commemorating the battle. To punish them for not rescuing his father, I suppose. He marked the tomb with the seal of a griffon."

"The crypt!" Moyra gasped. "That's the crypt we're looking for!"

Kellach told him about the key and explained Nimrae's plan. "The key is supposed to unlock the tomb. We must raise the dead Knights to fight Nimrae's ghost army. Do you know where we can find the tomb?"

Alaric shook his head. "I wish I did. My brave compatriots lie there. But I'm afraid I have never been able to find it. But I do know it is somewhere on Lord Dardley's hunting grounds."

"Rom was right!" Moyra jumped up. "It's in the forest. So we just have to search the game preserve until we find it!"

Kellach withdrew the key from his pouch and placed it in Alaric's palm. "Do you know what the patterns on the key represent?"

Alaric massaged the engraved circle and ray symbol with his fingertips. "It feels a bit like a wheel," he said. "This is the hub and these are the spokes." He flipped the key and felt the griffon. "And this represents the griffon that guards the crypt."

Moyra stiffened. "The griffon is still alive?"

"Moonshadow has seen signs," the Knight replied. "Bones where it has fed—"

"Why would a monster hang around a bunch of dead Knights?" Driskoll asked.

"Because the tomb lies in its lair."

Kellach gave a low whistle. "This makes things even worse. If we find the crypt, how are we going to get past this blood-thirsty beast?"

"If you are true Knights of the Silver Dragon, I am sure you will find a way." Alaric stood, waking Moonshadow. "Come, Moonshadow. It is time the Seekers return to Curston." Moonshadow began to lead Alaric away.

"Wait! We're lost!" Driskoll cried.

The old Knight called over his shoulder. "Take the right fork."

Moyra looked at Kellach and smirked. "I told you so."

CHAPTER

11

The right fork led them to another path that eventually brought them to Lord Dardley's private gate. It was open. The last of the hunting party straggled in from the opposite direction. The meat cart rattled across the gravel. It was empty. The dogs' tails drooped. Even the horses walked despondently.

"They didn't catch anything," Moyra said. "Not even a squirrel."

"That proves they were after Moonshadow," Driskoll said. "Or they would have stayed out longer."

"I wonder what this means for Dad?" said Moyra. "If the hunt was a failure, will he be let go?"

Lady Caroline cantered into the courtyard, and led her horse away from her father's admirers. She pulled up near the kids, dismounted, and lifted her mare's foreleg.

"Wat told me about the white wolf," she said, pretending to pick a stone from her horse's hoof. "More of Nimrae's work?"

"He's friendly," said Kellach. "Belongs to Alaric, who was in the battle in which your grandfather died."

Lady Caroline paused. "Someone actually *survived* that horrible battle? Does he know the location of the crypt?"

"No," Moyra answered. "But he says it's in the game preserve."

"We'll find it," Driskoll said confidently.

"Two more days," Lady Caroline reminded them. She swung up onto the saddle and cantered away.

A man broke through the crowd. It was Breddo. When he caught sight of Moyra, he strode over and picked her up.

"Hey, there, how's my girl!" he said, with a broad grin splitting his face.

"Daddy! Put me down!" But she enjoyed her father's display of affection. "Did you like being on the hunt today?"

"It was grand! Simply grand! Moyra, my girl, you're looking at a future huntsman." He pointed to himself.

"Really?"

"Lord Dardley's huntsmen said I was a fine beater. They want me to stay on. If I work hard, I can be a huntsman some day." He dug into his pocket. "Look! I got a bonus!" He held up two copper pieces.

"Oh, Daddy!" Moyra beamed with happiness.

He pressed a copper into her hand. "Some Travelers are over there with their wares. Treat yourself and the boys to a crumb-bun."

"Thanks, Breddo," Kellach said.

"Thanks a lot," said Driskoll.

Moyra flung her arms around her father's neck. Then she was off, racing across the green. Kellach and Driskoll sprinted to keep up with her.

A few Travelers had set up a tent. One man played a pipe. Another was selling crumb-buns.

A young woman in scarlet and yellow skirts stood beside a wooden Wheel of Fortune that was at least six feet tall. The wheel was divided into nine sections, alternately painted red and yellow. Fortunes, such as "happiness," "wealth," and "marriage," were written in the pie-shaped sections. Along the rim of the wheel were thin metal posts, like spokes.

The woman smiled at Moyra. "Copper a spin, young miss. Find out what the future holds for you."

"Don't waste your money, Moyra," said Kellach.

The woman narrowed her eyes at him.

But Moyra was so glad her father had found a job he might be good at that she *wanted* to spend a copper on something frivolous.

"Will I have good fortune?" she asked the woman.

The woman smiled, though the smile didn't reach her eyes. "Only the wheel can tell you."

Kellach plucked at her sleeve. "Let's get back to town."

"Kellach, don't be such a spoilsport." She handed the Traveler her coin.

"The young lady has crossed my palm," said the woman, throwing Kellach a dark look.

Moyra grabbed the wheel with both hands and spun it so hard that her feet lifted from the ground.

The wheel went round and round, vigorously at first, then with less energy as the wooden dowel clicked against the metal spokes. *Ticka-ticka-ticka.* Light flashed between the spokes.

Moyra was mesmerized by the flickering image. She kept thinking of what Alaric had said about the key. The pattern showed a wheel. But where would they find a wheel in the forest . . .

With a few final *tick-ticks*, the wheel landed on the line between "happiness" and "troubles ahead."

"Oh! Look how close you came!" the woman said. "I'm sure you'll get a good fortune with another spin."

"Not another copper for your lies!" Kellach said hotly. "Come on." He and Driskoll left.

Moyra stared hard at the wheel as if willing it to move to "happiness." But, of course, it didn't budge. As she turned to follow Kellach and Driskoll, she caught the eye of the young woman.

The smooth, unlined face of the young Traveler suddenly became as wrinkled as wadded parchment. Bluish green veins webbed from amber eyes. A hairy spider spun a silken thread from her crooked nose to a wart on her prominent chin. The young woman had turned into a hag!

For a full minute, she stared into the dark orange iris. It was like falling into a swirling fiery pool. She saw an image of herself being consumed by flames, her mouth open in a silent scream.

Then she heard someone say: *You belong to me* . . .

A gust of wind kicked up. It toppled awnings and knocked over tables, shaking Moyra out of her vision.

The Traveler woman's skirts blew up, revealing her calves and knees. Before she pushed them down again in embarrassment, Moyra noticed something odd about her legs.

Her calves were hairy and muscular. Like a man's.

"What are *you* looking at?" The hag was gone and the young Traveler was back. "Don't you have any manners?"

Moyra jerked her gaze away. Sweat popped out on her forehead from the intense heat of the flames in her vision.

"Um—excuse me!" Moyra whirled and ran through the crowd of hunters. She caught up to Kellach and Driskoll.

"Boys! Wait! The strangest thing just happened." She told them about her vision and the bizarre woman. "The wind blew her skirts up and I saw her legs. They were *muscular*, like a man's."

Driskoll shrugged. "She probably rides horses. It's harder to control a horse riding sidesaddle than astride."

"Only women of noble birth ride sidesaddle," Kellach informed him. "But there's something definitely odd about that woman. We should go ask Zendric. He's probably feeling better by now."

Driskoll nodded. "Good idea. We can tell him about Alaric. Maybe now that we know the crypt is in the game preserve, he'll be able to help us find it."

$$\blacksquare \quad \blacksquare \quad \blacksquare \quad \blacksquare \quad \blacksquare$$

They rushed back down the Oldgate Highway, through the city to the Wizards' Quarter, and up the steps to Zendric's tower.

Moyra gazed around the main room. No sign of Zendric.

"Zendric?" Kellach called.

Then Moyra noticed a sprawl of clothes on the floor.

"Zendric?" she whispered.

The pile of clothes twitched.

CHAPTER

12

"Zendric!" Driskoll cried. "Did he fall? Is he hurt? Is he breathing?"

Kellach bent down and put his ear on the wizard's chest. "He's breathing, but his heartbeat is weak. Let's get him off the floor."

Kellach picked up his legs while Driskoll and Moyra each took a shoulder. Together, they lifted the old elf onto the armchair in front of the hearth. Zendric did not move or open his eyes.

Moyra covered Zendric with a blanket. "He doesn't weigh more than a cat. Kell, I'm afraid he might die! What are we going to do?"

"We could summon Latislav to heal him," said Driskoll. "He's the cleric. Can't he do something?"

"I think we need to keep Zendric's illness a secret. We don't want Nimrae to find out." Kellach glanced around at the litter of bottles and jars on the worktable. "I could make a potion—but that would mean searching through Zendric's books for the right one. And that takes time."

"We don't have time," Driskoll pointed out. "Zendric needs help *now*."

"What about Lady Caroline?" Moyra suggested. "She healed your scratch, remember?"

"Perfect. We know she'll be discreet," Kellach said. "You're the fastest. Run back to Dardley Hall and fetch her."

Moyra sprinted out the door without further urging.

Soon she was back at Dardley Hall. The festive mood of the hunting party had subsided. The green was deserted. The Travelers and their tent was gone, and the Wheel of Fortune along with it.

The forbidding gates were now closed. The guard on the other side paced back and forth, his lance over his shoulder.

Just beyond, she saw Lady Caroline and her maid picking herbs.

Moyra ducked into the bushes near the wall. She couldn't very well demand to see Lady Caroline. No guard in his right mind would let a rogue girl onto the estate grounds.

She scrabbled around her feet until her fingers closed over a nice-sized stone. She had one shot—she'd better not miss it.

When the guard shifted his lance, she stood up quickly and lobbed the stone. It soared over the wall and landed in Lady Caroline's path.

Lady Caroline frowned, then looked thoughtful. "Dudley," she called to the guard. "I thought I heard something by the chicken house. Would you go check?"

Dudley marched around to the back of the manor house.

Lady Caroline hurried to the gate. "Moyra! What's wrong?"

"It's Zendric. Oh, Lady Caroline, he might die! We need your help."

"I'll be just two minutes," she said.

It was more than two minutes, but not many, before Lady Caroline appeared on her mare, a satchel strapped to her horse. Her maid Mary followed on a shaggy pony.

Lady Caroline opened the gate and they rode out.

"Moyra, get on behind Mary," Lady Caroline said. Moyra hesitated. "It's all right. The pony can easily carry your weight. Riding will be faster."

On horseback, they arrived at Zendric's in no time. Kellach opened the door with obvious relief and dashed out to help Lady Caroline dismount.

"Thank you for coming, my lady."

"Moyra was most insistent. Mary, bring my satchel." Hoisting her long skirts, Lady Caroline hurried into Zendric's house.

With one glance at Zendric's parchment-pale face on the pillow, she knelt by the armchair. The others stood around in a semicircle.

"Zendric," Lady Caroline said sweetly into his ear. "Can you hear me?"

The wizard did not speak. He did not move.

Mary examined Zendric and whispered something in Lady Caroline's ears.

Lady Caroline looked up at Kellach. "Has Nimrae been here?"

"Nimrae? Why would he—?" Then he remembered. "Yes! Zendric said Nimrae came on a 'social visit.' But nothing happened."

Lady Caroline exchanged a horrified glance with Mary. "That was it then."

Mary nodded.

"What?" Moyra asked. "What are you talking about?"

Lady Caroline sighed. "Mary believes Nimrae left a present."

"Zendric didn't say anything about a present," said Kellach. "What kind of a present?"

"A poppet," Mary spoke up. "Zendric wouldn't have known about it. Nimrae planted it somewhere in Zendric's house."

"What's a poppet?" asked Moyra.

"A sort of charm," Mary explained. "Poppets are made in the person's image. The person grows weaker and weaker, until they become like a puppet commanded by the wizard who created the poppet."

Kellach's eyes widened. "But how could Nimrae do this to Zendric? He's the strongest wizard in all of Curston."

"I'm not sure," said Lady Caroline. "Maybe Nimrae plans

to weaken Zendric so he can't help you three on this quest."

"Then let's look for this poppet thing," Driskoll said.

Lady Caroline leaned over Zendric's face and placed her hand against his forehead. "Cool," she pronounced. "He's not feverish. Has he been in his right mind?"

"Zendric has the sharpest mind of anyone I know," Kellach said firmly.

"Don't take offense. This illness doesn't just affect the body." Lady Caroline set her satchel on the worktable and opened it. She pulled out several vials of herbs and turned to her maid. "What do you think, Mary?"

Mary frowned. "Not broom—he's not yellow, so I don't think his kidneys are ailing. Put that poppy away too. He doesn't have a toothache." She nodded at the last three vials. "Coltsfoot is good. He could have a chest ailment. So is foxglove—his heart skips. But I think that one alone may do the trick." She pointed to the last vial.

"What is it?" Moyra asked, still leery.

"Willow and peony root," Lady Caroline replied. "Peony is said to keep away evil spirits and cure lunacy—just in case, Kellach. The root is highly poisonous and shrieks if dug up. Anyone nearby is doomed to instant death. So Mary and I tied one of the manor dogs to the root and let him pull it out."

Kellach was alarmed. "Won't it kill Zendric?"

"No. I'll make a decoction using just the right amount." She patted his arm. "Don't fret. I've done this before."

Moyra told him, "We have no choice, Kell."

"If Zendric dies . . . ," Kellach whispered.

"No one is going to die," Lady Caroline said. "Kellach, I need a clean cloth."

While Kellach ripped a towel into small rags and Lady Caroline prepared the medicine, Driskoll and Moyra searched for the poppet. They peeked under the furniture, peered behind tapestries, and shook the folds of the brocade drapes.

"There's a lot of strange stuff," Driskoll reported. "But I don't see anything that could be an image of him."

Lady Caroline poured the decoction into a cup and took it to Zendric. She tucked a clean rag in the collar of his robes.

"Get behind him and push him up," she told Kellach. "I don't want him to choke."

Kellach and Mary held the wizard by his arms. Moyra thought it was like handling a rag doll. Except for his shallow breathing and faint heartbeat, Zendric seemed to have passed into the world beyond.

Lady Caroline placed the cup against Zendric's mouth. "Open wide," she coaxed, as if talking to a small child. The wizard's lips parted a fraction. The cup clinked against his teeth and liquid dribbled down his chin, but Lady Caroline was able to get some of the medicine down his throat.

Kellach and Mary laid him back. After a few moments, color returned to Zendric's face. He opened his eyes and blinked.

"Oh, Zendric!" Kellach exclaimed. "We were so worried—"

"Give the medicine a chance to work, Kellach," Lady Caroline said. "Zendric is very weak. He'll need some time before he can talk. His mind may be cloudy too."

"No, it isn't," Zendric croaked, clearly in control of his senses. "Lady Caroline . . . the last time I saw you, you were in short skirts."

She blushed. "Well, I'm all grown up now."

"I can see that," Zendric said hoarsely. "You probably saved my life. What was in that horrible drink, by the way?"

"Never mind." Lady Caroline packed her satchel. "I pulled you through this episode, but you're far from cured." She explained her theory about the poppet.

Zendric waved a weak hand. "Nonsense. Nimrae isn't clever enough to fool me with a poppet." Zendric turned to Kellach, Driskoll, and Moyra. "What progress have you made in finding the crypt?"

Driskoll stepped up. "Not much, but we have learned a lot of new things." Driskoll began to fill Zendric and Lady Caroline in on all they'd learned so far—how they'd met Moonshadow and Alaric.

"Alaric! Alive?" Zendric shook his head. "Amazing. He was one of the most valiant Knights I've ever known. You can trust him, my friends. Use his knowledge. Let him help you."

Lady Caroline put her hand on Driskoll's arm. "I don't think Zendric is up for much more discussion. But someone should stay with him to give him the rest of the medicine. I'd do it, but my father is giving a banquet tonight for the huntsmen, and I must rush back."

"There isn't anybody but us," Kellach said. "And we have to find the crypt."

"I'll stay," Mary offered. She cast a critical eye around the room. "The place could do with a bit of tidying too."

"Don't go messing with my things!" Zendric said, struggling to sit up.

"Relax," Lady Caroline told him. "Mary will only be here until curfew."

She turned to Kellach. Her expression was serious.

"Two more days. Do you think you'll find it?"

"Of course," Kellach said confidently.

Moyra exchanged a worried look with Driskoll. She hoped Kellach was right.

Lady Caroline simply nodded. "Nimrae will be at the banquet, gloating by my father's elbow, as usual. He may let a nugget of news slip. If he does, I'll hear him." Lady Caroline issued final instructions to Mary on Zendric's care, then left.

Mary went into the kitchen, mumbling about dirty dishes.

"What are we going to do now?" Driskoll asked, flopping onto the armchair next to Zendric, who had fallen fast asleep.

Kellach scrunched his nose, a sign he was thinking. "Let's go over the clues we have so far." Kellach pulled the key out of the pouch on his belt and stared at the wheel-like symbol. "Alaric said that this side of the key looks like a wheel."

Driskoll leaned forward. "And he said that the crypt is somewhere in Lord Dardley's hunting grounds."

"In the griffon's lair." Kellach flipped the key over and stared at the other side with the griffon symbol.

"Sounds like a whole lot of nothing to me." Moyra flopped down next to Driskoll. "The only thing I can think of doing is searching all of Lord Dardley's land. But that would take weeks! We don't have that kind of time." Moyra looked down. "If only we could find someone who knew where the crypt was . . . someone who could just show it to us."

Kellach seemed mesmerized by the griffon symbol on the key. He stared at it for a long time, then slowly began to nod his head. "There is someone who knows where the crypt is."

"There is?" Moyra brightened. "Who?"

Kellach held up the key. "The griffon."

Driskoll laughed. "Are you saying we should go griffon hunting?"

Kellach grinned. "That's *exactly* what we're going to do!"

"I was just kidding!" Driskoll said.

"Well, I'm not kidding," his brother returned. "Alaric said the crypt was in the griffon's lair. Instead of fumbling around trying to find the crypt, we'll let the griffon *take* us to it."

"You do remember that the griffon attacked Alaric and blinded him," Moyra said.

"The griffon attacked Alaric by accident," Kellach said. "He was really after Ajax."

"Who?" asked Driskoll.

"Alaric's horse. Griffons are mortal enemies of horses, remember?"

"They aren't exactly best friends to humans either," Moyra said.

"Any better ideas?" Kellach threw back.

Moyra shrugged. They had accepted the mission aware of its dangers. But if they did nothing, the alternative was worse.

CHAPTER

13

With Moyra in the lead, the kids took a shortcut to Broken Town. They needed supplies to go griffon hunting, and Moyra's house was the closest.

Moyra's mother was home. She didn't seem pleased when they barged into her house, but made no comment when Moyra filled a pack with bread and a goatskin of water. She picked up a lantern off the table and took two of Breddo's ropes from a hook by the door.

"Here," she said, giving a coil of rope to Kellach. "Dad won't mind if we borrow these."

"Are you sure?" Kellach asked.

"He won't be around to miss 'em," Royma said heavily.

Moyra turned to her mother. "What do you mean? Hasn't he been home yet? Didn't he bring you his wages? The hunt is over."

Moyra's mother clucked her tongue. "Where is your father most evenings?"

Nobody answered. They didn't have to. Breddo's reputation for spending all his time and money in the Skinned Cat was well known.

"Maybe he's working late," Moyra mumbled. "The head huntsman could have kept him on to do other things."

But her bright happiness had dimmed. She wanted so much for her father to be a success, even in an honorable job.

■ ■ ▐ ■ ▐

Loaded with supplies, they left Curston through the Oldgate. On the road to Dardley Hall, they stopped and ate a quick meal. Then they started off once more. The road was ominously empty.

At Dardley Hall, the kids crept up to the now-open gates. Grooms were exercising the horses. Wat was currying Lord Dardley's chestnut stallion.

"At least the gates are open again," Moyra muttered. "All we have to do is get to the back door and head out into the hunting grounds."

"But there are too many people," Kellach muttered. "I don't see how we'll make it around to the back gate this time."

"Where is Lady Caroline when we need her?" Driskoll asked.

"Maybe her father is becoming harder to handle," Moyra

said. She knew all too well what it was like to have a less-than-perfect father.

"Into the bushes," Kellach said. "*Now!*"

They hurried inside the bushes, keeping as close to the wall as possible. Driskoll was so busy watching the grooms that he didn't pay attention to where he was going. He snagged his toe on a root and tripped.

"Get up!" Kellach whispered.

Someone was coming toward them. Driskoll scrambled to get up. Just then the bushes were thrust apart, and a familiar face grinned down at them.

"Oh!" Wat said, his grin stretching. "Master Kellach!"

"Hey, Wat!" one of the grooms called. "What are you doing? Smellin' the roses?"

"Wat!" Moyra whispered. "Don't give us away!"

"Lost me button," Wat yelled.

"That's not all you lost," the man said with a guffaw.

Wat got down on his hands and knees and pretended to search. "M'lady say hurry."

"We *are* hurrying," Driskoll said. "We're trying to get out the back gate."

Kellach clutched Wat's arm. "Did Lady Caroline say anything else?"

Moyra hushed him. "The grooms are coming over here!" she said. "Move it!"

"I help." Wat scampered out of the bushes and back to the

horses. Suddenly he flung himself on the ground and began moaning. He arched his back as if in terrible pain.

The grooms changed course and rushed to him. One of the men stood up, as if to leave. Wat moaned louder.

Moyra caught a glimpse of the man before he disappeared into the group. There was something familiar about the set of his shoulders. Was that her dad? She couldn't tell for sure through the shrubbery, and Kellach was beckoning to her. She hurried on.

While Lord Dardley's men were occupied, Kellach, Moyra, and Driskoll raced around the back to the door leading into the game preserve. The guard had been called away to assist with Wat, so once more they were in luck.

They ran down the main path until they were half a mile away from the walls of Dardley Hall. As they ran, the trees grew taller and closer together. The sky darkened as the foliage canopy blocked out the sun. Goose bumps rose on Moyra's arms. Would the griffon come and get them?

All at once, Kellach stopped beside a tall oak tree. He stood on the path, panting.

"What are you going to do?" Driskoll asked nervously.

Kellach turned until his back was against the tree. As he chanted, he reached into his pouch and pulled out a white hair. He swung the hair through the air in an intricate pattern, and just as he finished the incantation, he flicked it away.

The hair disappeared, and a stallion stood in its place.

Moyra took a step back in awe. The creature Kellach conjured was beautiful, at least eighteen hands high, with a golden coat and silvery mane and tail. The horse seemed created from sunlight and moonbeams. He bent his elegant neck and nibbled at blades of grass growing at the base of the tree.

"Oh, Kellach," Moyra breathed, enchanted. "Is he ours? Are we going to ride him?"

"No," Kellach said flatly. "He's bait."

"Bait?" And then she understood. "NO!"

But it was too late.

The atmosphere suddenly shuddered, became turbulent. The leaves on the trees turned inside out, as if a huge storm was headed their way. The wind strengthened to hurricane force. Driskoll backed against a tree trunk to keep from being blown over.

Kellach yelled over the wind. "Get ready to run!"

Moyra stood firm. "Forget it, Kell. We're not leaving you alone."

Green darkness swirled around them. Overhead, the trees swayed, and their branches rubbed together with a mournful sound.

From the darkness came a furious snarling and a searing heat. The sky parted as if rent by giant hands. *Whump!* A creature dropped into the clearing mere yards from the kids.

Taller than a house and as wide as St. Cuthbert's tower, the beast landed on four paws that ended in pearly, dagger-like claws.

Strong wings, sprouting from heavily muscled shoulders, beat the air. The long lion's tail, tipped with a golden tuft, flicked like a whip.

"Gods," Kellach whispered.

"If this is a dream," Driskoll said, awestruck, "I want to wake up."

Moyra made no comment but watched to see the griffon's intent. Would it tear out their throats or go for Kellach's magnificent horse?

Ignoring the kids, the griffon rose on its hind legs and snapped its wicked beak at the horse. Frightened, the horse reared, its whinny ending in a scream.

"Kellach!" Moyra cried. "It's going after the horse! Do something!"

"I didn't think the griffon would attack the horse so quickly," Kellach said, panicked. "I thought it would be curious about us, and I could communicate with it, get it to lead us to the crypt—"

"Never mind about that!" Moyra shouted. This was hardly the time to discuss his foolish plan.

The horse ran, but the griffon covered the ground between them in two bounds, its breath scorching the grass. The horse's screams were horrible.

Kellach screwed his eyes shut and chanted under his breath. Moyra prayed his intonation was exactly right.

The griffon coiled all its energy, ready to pounce, when the horse suddenly vanished in a vapor of silver-tinged gold.

The griffon blinked heavy-lidded yellow eyes in surprise. Then it turned on Kellach with a roar.

"I—I'll bring the horse back if you bring us to your lair," Kellach bargained.

The beast growled.

Moyra knew the beast could easily outrun them. Their only escape was up.

"Climb!" she shouted as the griffon sprang.

Moyra leaped, grabbing the nearest limb of the oak tree. She scrambled up the tree from handhold to handhold, Driskoll and Kellach close behind her.

They could feel the griffon's hot breath. It stood on its hind legs, waiting for one of them to stumble and fall into its gaping beak. Then it stretched its long wings, preparing to take flight.

Moyra's stomach sank. She had temporarily forgotten the beast could fly! It would pluck them out of the tree like a duck nipping ladybugs off a potato bush. They couldn't outrun or outclimb the griffon.

They were doomed.

She closed her eyes and waited for the razor-sharp beak to maul her flesh.

CHAPTER

14

Moyra felt the tree shiver and heard a low growl.

"Hey!" Driskoll cried from a branch below her. "Look!"

Moyra opened her eyes and saw a flurry of white. Moonshadow! The wolf had come to their rescue!

Moonshadow hurled himself at the griffon's hindquarters, his strong claws raking the griffon's flank. With a roar, the griffon wheeled, with its eagle eyes flashing. Then the griffon clamped its wicked beak on one of Moonshadow's front paws. The wolf howled, breaking the griffon's hold.

For minutes, all the kids could see was a blizzard of white fur and a flutter of feathered wings. It was hard to tell which animal was winning. The griffon's claws slashed, and Moonshadow's fangs dripped saliva as they locked in battle.

Then the great wolf twisted and leaped, landing on the griffon's back. All four paws dug into the griffon's hide. The griffon screeched—a sound so high-pitched and horrible that the kids had to cover their ears at the risk of falling out of the tree. Bigger than the wolf, the griffon used its size to advantage. It stood on its hind legs, buffeting Moonshadow with its wings. The wolf tumbled to the ground, momentarily stunned.

"Get up, Moonshadow!" Moyra yelled. She didn't care the wolf could only communicate with Kellach. If Moonshadow were hurt or killed . . .

The wolf did get up, shaking his massive jowls. The griffon was poised to attack again, tail thrashing from side to side. Moonshadow waited until the griffon sprang. As the huge beast arched in midair, the wolf lunged, sinking his fangs into the griffon's underbelly.

The griffon screamed again, this time in sheer agony. Oozing blood from its wounds, the beast flew off in defeat. The woods shook with its anguished cries.

When the creature was gone, the kids shinnied down the tree. Kellach landed lightly on the ground next to Moonshadow.

"How did you know we were in trouble?" he asked the wolf.

He paused while the wolf responded.

"What did he say?" Driskoll asked Kellach.

"Moonshadow said he came because Alaric sensed we were in trouble."

"We're glad he did. Thanks, Moonshadow." Driskoll held out his hand. The wolf hesitated only a second, then licked it gently. "His tongue feels rough, like sandstone."

"Now what?" Moyra asked Kellach. "Your plan didn't work. The griffon had no intention of leading us to the crypt or anywhere else except its stomach."

"You're mad because I used the horse as bait."

"Yes, I am! And furious because we were nearly killed!" Moyra's temper flared quickly but died down just as fast. "Sorry, Kell. You made the horse escape, so no harm was done to him."

Kellach didn't answer. He was staring at Moonshadow, nodding his head gravely.

"What did he say?" Moyra asked, watching the wolf lope away.

"He's going to track the griffon. Maybe find his lair," Kellach said. "But every time Moonshadow has tried to do that, the griffon has led him all over the forest."

"He might have better luck this time because the griffon is upset." Driskoll called after Moonshadow, "Be careful!"

"*We* should be following the griffon ourselves," Kellach said grimly. "In less than two days, Curston will crumble just like the Old City. Nimrae's army will wreak destruction if we don't find the crypt and raise the dead Knights."

Moyra nodded. Of all their missions—and they'd had some difficult ones—this was the ultimate challenge. No wonder Kellach was frustrated. They had made almost no progress. *Why couldn't they find the crypt?*

The tree beside them cast a long, gloomy shadow across the woods. Its round trunk echoed the hub of a wheel. And the shadows of the other trees were like the spokes.

"Kell," she said, an idea beginning to hatch in her mind, "let me see the key for a minute."

He pulled the silver key from his pouch and gave it to her. Her fingers traced the wheel design on the back. A map, Rom had insisted. A wheel, Alaric had determined. A map *and* a wheel.

"What are you thinking?" Kellach asked her.

"While I was up in the tree, I had a good view of the forest. I could see a lot of the trails and paths." She held up the key. "I think they make a pattern."

"Like the one on the key?" Driskoll asked hopefully.

"I'm not sure. I didn't get a good look. I was too busy trying to stay alive. But I bet if someone climbed even *higher*, that person could see *all* the trails."

She patted the trunk of the tree and looked up. Then she gave Driskoll her most winning smile.

He held up both hands. "Oh, no! I only climbed that tree to keep from being the main course at the griffon's banquet, same as you! I'm not going up there again, even if you point a sword at me!"

"Dris, you're the lightest," Moyra coaxed. "It makes sense for you to climb."

"Why?" He hated heights and tried to remain on firm ground

at all costs. "What am I looking for up there anyway?"

"The crypt," Kellach and Moyra answered together.

"You believe the crypt is in the tree?" Driskoll asked.

Moyra rolled her eyes. "Listen carefully. I think the paths reflect the design on the key. And that the crypt is in the center—the hub."

"You go," he said to Moyra. "You're the best tree climber."

"I can't," Moyra said. "I don't think those top branches will hold my weight. Come on, Driskoll, just do this one thing and I'll get—buy—you a crumb-bun. Two crumb-buns."

He looked suspicious. "I don't like that gleam in your eye. How dangerous is it?"

"Well, you'll have to climb to the very top of this tree. From there you'll be able to see all the paths and where they meet."

"Are you crazy?" Driskoll backed away as if to ward off an evil spell.

Kellach crossed his arms. "Do you want me to tell Zendric we failed to save Curston because you were too scared to—"

"All right!" Driskoll said. "*Three* crumb-buns with extra sugar."

"Deal!"

"I'll give you a boost," Kellach said. "You ready?"

Driskoll tipped his head back to take in the tree's full height. "Three crumb-buns may not be enough to risk my life," he muttered. "I'd rather visit the blacksmith and have a tooth yanked out."

Kellach laced his fingers together to make a stirrup. Driskoll put one boot in his brother's hands, and Kellach hoisted him up so Driskoll could grab the lowest branch.

He scrabbled up fairly quickly since the bottom branches were large and accessible. But he slowed as he worked his way up into the smaller branches.

"It's kind of creepy up here," he reported.

"Creepy how?" asked Moyra.

But before he could answer, a creature swooped out of the sky. Moyra couldn't see it very well, but it was about a foot long, with a huge wingspan.

Startled, Driskoll shrieked and slid down the trunk, catching himself barely in time. The bird flapped away with a series of high-pitched, unearthly cries.

"Dris?" Kellach called. "You all right?"

"I—I don't think I can do this," came his brother's quivery reply.

"You can do it," Moyra said.

"I'm too high!" His voice held an edge of panic.

"Don't look down," advised Kellach. "Or look up."

"I'm coming back down." Leaves stirred, marking his hasty descent. Soon Moyra saw his feet appear. He skinned down the trunk, his face pale as chalk.

"Are you all right?" Kellach asked. "That thing didn't hurt you, did it?"

Driskoll shook his head. "No, but it kept flying at me, like it wanted me *out* of the tree, or else it would make me get down. The hard way."

Moyra heaved a heavy sigh. "Fine. I guess I'll just have to do this myself."

Kellach and Driskoll boosted her to a strong, low-hanging branch. Moyra scrambled up the tree, quickly finding hand- and footholds. As she climbed, the branches became scrawnier. She carefully tested each branch before placing her whole weight on it. Down below, Kellach and Driskoll looked impossibly small, like chess pieces.

As she neared the top, her ears started buzzing. She stopped, hooking her right arm around the trunk. She shook her head like a goat shooing away flies. The buzzing persisted. Then it disappeared as suddenly as it had come, only to be replaced by soft lyrical sounds, like music played by fairies on midsummer's eve. Pleasant. Lulling. Persuasive.

"Can you see anything yet?" Kellach yelled up to her.

His voice came to her like harp notes on the wind.

She paid him no attention. Up this high, she could see the entire world, it seemed. Oaks and poplars, chestnuts and laurel trees stretched away to all four corners.

The landscape was bisected and crisscrossed by curving bridle paths: some wide and some no more than rabbit trails. Most of the paths led into other paths. All but one. One path cut purposely through the forest, ending at a grassy mound.

Suddenly a great hawk burst from the sky. Its enormous gray wings flapped rapidly for several beats, then it glided, swooping around Moyra's head.

Music swelled inside her brain. The wings of the great bird seemed to be playing the music, each beat a new chord, harmonizing with the soft breeze. Moyra leaned into the sweet sound, taking her arm from around the tree trunk.

Then she heard someone say: *You belong to me, remember?*

Her right foot skidded off the branch. Her hands grabbed for the trunk but met only air.

CHAPTER

15

Moyra tumbled through the boughs, stripping leaves from branches, with her arms windmilling in a futile attempt to break her fall. Twigs ripped her clothes and clawed her face and hands. She did not notice the pain. She did not utter a sound.

She experienced no fear, only the sensation of wafting like a milkweed seed. Any second, she imagined, she would take flight like the elegant swans that sometimes flew over Curston.

From below, she heard Kellach faintly calling her name. But the voice persisted.

You will do my bidding . . .

"Moy-ra!" Kellach's voice broke in.

Her survival instinct finally kicked in. Suddenly she did not feel like an elegant swan. More like a baby bird shoved from its nest by a bigger sibling. Using her last ounce of strength, she dug her fingers into the rough bark of the trunk. She gripped the trunk with her knees, still sliding. Her fall slowed and eventually stopped.

She clung to the tree, panting. Her fingertips bled, the knees of her pants bristled with splinters, and her kneecaps were scraped raw. She was alive but could not move. Moyra squinched her eyes shut, still feeling a sickening plunge in her stomach. She began to shake uncontrollably.

"I'm coming up!" said Kellach.

The other voice faded to a hateful hiss.

Then Kellach was beside her on the tree with one arm hanging over a branch for safety. "You can let go now." He gently pried her fingers away from the trunk. "I'll help you down." He showed her where to place her feet and hands.

Slowly, Moyra climbed down the rest of the way. When they were on the ground, Driskoll ran over. "Oh, Moyra! You're hurt!" He ripped a corner off his tunic and dabbed at her scratches with it.

"Moyra," said Kellach, peering at her. "What happened up there? What made you fall?"

Moyra simply stared at her hands as Driskoll wiped off the blood. The voice in her head returned, more persuasive than ever.

I will take you and your family someplace special . . . you will never want again . . .

If Moyra just gave into it, she could forget all her cares. She wouldn't have to look for—what was it she was hunting for? No matter. The voice was promising her a better, easier life, if only she would—

"Did you hear me?" Kellach said. "What *happened*?"

Moyra could not reply. It was as if her lips had been stitched closed.

Driskoll passed his hand several times before her eyes. She blinked in response.

"She can see," Driskoll said. Next he snapped his fingers in front of her face. She blinked again. "And hear. Moyra," he said loudly, "answer us!"

Moyra looked past him into nothingness. She was aware of her chest rising and falling, aware of the soles of her boots meeting the ground. In her mind, she was searching for the place the voice had promised to take her to, a place where she and her parents would be happy always and forever.

Kellach grabbed Moyra by the shoulders. "Her eyes look weird, kind of blank."

"Maybe the griffon scared her into this . . . this state," Driskoll said.

"I doubt it. Moyra's as tough as a troll's foot." Kellach peered closely into Moyra's face.

"What's wrong with her?" Driskoll asked.

"I think she's been enchanted," Kellach looked back at his brother. "That bird you saw when you were up there. What did it look like?"

Driskoll shrugged. "Some kind of hawk. With giant gray wings."

"The goshawk," Kellach said. "Nimrae's familiar. Nimrae used his familiar to cast the spell over her while she was up in that tree. But if he could do it to Moyra, why didn't he try the same thing on you?"

"I don't know." Driskoll shrugged his shoulder. "It must mean Moyra saw something up there. We must be getting close to finding the crypt. Nimrae's desperate to stop us."

"But we won't know where to look until Moyra tells us." Kellach sighed.

"Let's take her to Zendric," Driskoll suggested. "He'll know what to do."

"He's not in very good shape," Kellach said. "I'm not sure he'll be able to help us."

Moyra heard the exchange as if through wads of cotton. The muffled conversation meant nothing to her.

"What are we going to do?" Driskoll asked.

Kellach stood up. "We're just going to have to fix her up ourselves." He pulled the waterskin out of Moyra's pack. "First, clean Moyra's scrapes."

Driskoll soaked the scrap of torn tunic in the water and washed sticky dried blood off Moyra's hands and knees.

Moyra did not turn her head. She sat woodenly on the ground.

"This water has to sting," he said. "But she doesn't even wince. It's like she's a puppet."

Kellach frowned. "Nimrae seems to like to turn his victims into puppets. Remember what Mary said? That poppet thing will turn Zendric into a puppet too."

"We can't let Moyra end up like Zendric!"

"We're not going to. Now stand back."

Kellach cupped Moyra's chin in his hand, staring deeply into her eyes. Without looking away, he whispered under his breath and traced a gesture in the air with his free hand. For a moment, Moyra's hair seemed to glow with an unnatural white light. At first, the halo of light seemed to shimmer.

Moyra's skin tingled. She almost felt like she could open her mouth to speak . . .

Then with a sharp popping sound, the light fizzled into the air.

Kellach jerked his hand back. "Ow!"

Driskoll rushed back to Moyra's side and prodded her shoulder. "Moyra? Are you all right?"

Moyra didn't move.

Driskoll looked up at his brother. "It didn't work!"

Kellach grunted. "I know. That's a really hard spell. Something went wrong."

"Great. What are we going to do now? We can't just leave her like this." Driskoll plopped back down on the ground, his chin in his hands. The platinum ring on his index finger caught the sunlight.

Kellach's eyes flew wide. "Dris, that's it!"

"What's it?" Driskoll said glumly.

Kellach pointed at his brother's index finger. "The platinum ring. That's the one you bought from Mary, right? That's why the goshawk's spell didn't affect you. It reverses enchantments, remember? Quickly—"

Kellach grabbed his brother's finger and started pulling on the ring.

"Hey!" Driskoll cried. "You're hurting me. I can do that myself!" He wrenched his hand out of his brother's and pulled the band off.

He turned to Moyra. Lifting her floppy right hand, he slid the band onto her index finger. Although Driskoll's fingers were much smaller than Moyra's, the ring seemed to alter its shape to fit.

For a moment, nothing happened.

Driskoll stared at Moyra. "Do you think it's going to work?"

Kellach clenched his fists. "It's a strong spell. It may take a moment."

"Hey!" Driskoll said. "Her lips moved!"

Moyra opened her mouth once, then twice. She blinked again. After a moment, her blinking became more natural. She tried to rub away the film that veiled her eyes, then noticed her hands were bandaged. Her vision focused. She swallowed.

Licking her dry lips, she croaked, "Water—please."

Driskoll helped her take a drink out of the waterskin. "How do you feel?"

"Fine," she said slowly. "Well, sort of draggy. Like I've been watching everything you were doing through a thick obscuring mist."

"That feeling should be gone before tomorrow. And your hands will be better before tomorrow." Kellach winked. "Compliments of the house."

She gave him a faint smile. "Thanks. Hey! I'm hungry!"

Kellach laughed. "I guess that means you're back to normal!" He pulled out the bread from Moyra's pack and handed it to her.

She took another sip of water, then ripped off a chunk of bread before handing it back to Kellach.

Moyra felt tingly all over, every nerve alive and taut. Images flashed through her mind like shards of broken pottery. She saw an ever-shifting mosaic of purple robes, blue sky, and green leaves. Then the pieces emerged into a startling picture.

A path, one path from many, stabbed through the thick green forest, aiming toward a grassy mound.

"Kellach," she blurted. "I know where we can find the crypt!"

He leaped to his feet. "You saw it from the tree?"

"Clearly." She pointed up at the tall oak tree. "From up there, it *looked* like all the paths were spokes of a wheel," Moyra said. "But only one path leads to the center—the hub. The rest connected with other paths and ended before they reached the middle. If that makes sense."

"Do you remember which path goes to the center?" Kellach asked. "I mean, from the main bridle path outside Lord Dardley's back gate?"

She shook her head. "Sorry."

"It's all right." Kellach sighed. "I knew it wouldn't be that easy. But we've lost so much time now. We have to keep looking. Moyra, do you want to stay here and wait for us?"

She drew herself up to stand. "No way! You need me—I might recognize the right trail."

Kellach drew his knife. "I'll mark the paths we've been on so we don't follow them twice." He carved a *K* in the tall tree's trunk. "Our very own *patrin*."

The kids set off down the main path. When it forked, they found another trail and followed it to its end too.

Soon darkness was closing in.

"We must have walked a hundred trails," Driskoll said, yawning.

"More like fifteen or sixteen." Kellach inspected a tree to see if it was branded with his mark. "We've covered all the trails but this one. This trail *has* to be it."

They started down the path, careful not to noisily scuff old dead leaves. An owl swooped before them, dangling a shrew in its talons. Its wings brushed Moyra's cheek. The primary feathers smelled musty, like Zendric's old books. The shrew squeaked once, then was silent.

"I don't like these woods," Driskoll remarked.

Moyra nodded. "The trees keep secrets. It seems like all the power of life and death is in this forest."

"Since when are you so philosophical?" Driskoll said.

Kellach asked, "Moyra, do you remember this trail at all?"

Moyra nodded slowly. "Yes . . . Yes! I think this is the one. This leads directly to the mound."

A memory blazed across her brain. Someone calling her . . . *You belong to me* . . .

"Look out!" Kellach cried.

Moyra jumped back just in time to see an enormous ash tree falling through the trees. It was headed directly for Driskoll.

CHAPTER

16

Crash!

The ash tree fell across the path, just missing Driskoll by inches. The tree settled with a sigh, rustling its branches.

Driskoll jumped back. "Wow! That was close!"

Moyra stared up at the ancient tree. Its massive trunk was twice her height. A thicket of barbed branches created an impenetrable armor. "We've got to find some way to get past this. But there's no end to this thing!" She turned to Kellach. "Don't you know some kind of spell we could try?"

Kellach paced up and down, rubbing his chin. "I'm thinking."

"It's too bad we don't have an axe," Driskoll said wistfully.

Moyra was staring past them, down the path. "Be careful what you wish for."

A brawny man wearing browns and greens of a woodsman came toward them. His mane of bushy brown hair brushed against the axe he carried over one shoulder. Its wickedly sharp blade glinted in the last of the light of the day.

"Help ye?" The woodsman's growly voice sounded muffled through his thick brown beard.

Moyra didn't trust him. He reminded her of someone, but she couldn't think who.

Kellach spoke right up. "I don't suppose you could chop a section out of that tree. We need to get on the other side of the path, pretty quick."

The woodsman lowered his axe and leaned against the handle as if he had all the time in the world. "What's in it fer me?"

Kellach turned his pocket inside out. "I don't have any money, as you can see. But if you'll do us this favor, you'll be paid handsomely. My father is Torin, captain of the watch in Curston."

"City folk," the woodsman sneered. "Helpless as just-hatched goblins."

"We are not helpless!" Driskoll protested. "For your information, you happen to be looking at—"

"—three kids who need to get around this tree somehow," Kellach said, giving his brother a squelching look. "We would be much obliged if you would help us."

Moyra was still staring at the woodsman. His arm muscles bulged in his patched brown tunic. But his shoulders were bowed like a worn ox yoke. If the man earned his trade by swinging a heavy axe, wouldn't his shoulders match his arms?

She raised her gaze to his face. The woodsman was staring back at her.

"Like what ye see?" he demanded.

Moyra wasn't disarmed by his harsh tone. She did not look away.

His eyes. Black as obsidian chips and twice as hard. Where had she seen those eyes before?

"Well?" Kellach said. "Do we have a deal? My father will pay you whatever you ask if you chop a section out of this tree, but you *must* hurry."

"I don't know . . ." The man stroked his beard with one hand as if he enjoyed toying with them.

Moyra watched him intently. His biceps should have flexed with the motion. But it remained suspiciously flabby.

Suddenly she reached over and squeezed his upper arm. He jerked back, but Moyra hung onto the shabby sleeve. The fabric gave way, revealing a strip of linen bandage around his upper arm. Beneath the linen strips his arms were stick thin. Before he could react, Moyra ripped the other sleeve. More linen strips padded his arm, making the muscles appear bigger.

"Your muscles are fake!" she cried. "You're a fraud!"

Driskoll gave a harsh laugh. "That axe is just for show, just like your fake muscles."

"I don't know who you are or why you're dressed like that," Kellach said. "But I doubt you could wrestle your way out of a burlap sack. Now if you don't mind, we need to borrow your axe—"

The man raised the axe over his head. The blade collected all the light from the dying day and threw it back in a mighty blaze. *Zap!* A jagged lightning bolt sliced through the trunk of the tree like a branding iron through butter. A section of the tree, thicker than the three kids combined, vanished, leaving behind a small mountain of sizzling sawdust.

He turned to the kids, his face lit with the intensity of a brilliant madman. "*Now* what do you think of my puny muscles!"

"No mere man possesses such power. Who *are* you?" Kellach demanded.

For an answer, the man threw back his head and laughed.

"*Aha-ha-ha-ha-ha!*" He stopped to wipe a tear from his eye. "This is rich! I couldn't have planned it better!" He laughed so hard that he stumbled backward into a jutting branch and sat down hard on the ground.

His pants hiked up as he got back to his feet. Moyra recognized that hairy calf. The last time she saw that leg, it was swathed in red and yellow skirts.

"You're the Traveler with the Wheel of Fortune!" she accused.

"Right again," said the man, lifting his leg in a dancer's pose. Then he waved his hand over his face. When he removed it, he wore the hag face.

Driskoll stomped forward. "You gave Moyra bad fortunes!"

"I did nothing of the sort. I don't have to dabble in such whims," the man said, getting nimbly to his feet. "The rogue girl's fortunes were accurate. Is it her fault her father is—shall we say, less than a solid citizen?"

Moyra charged forward, fists clenched, but Kellach pulled her back.

"Don't play his game," he told her. To the woodsman he said, "Fool, Traveler woman, whatever. You still couldn't have done what you just did without sorcery."

The man leered at him. "You're all so smart, figuring out my disguises. But you missed the most important disguise of all."

Then Moyra noticed something that froze her blood. The felled tree cast a long shadow across the clearing.

The man did not.

"You have no shadow," she murmured.

Without changing his clothes or even moving, the woodsman emanated yet another persona. His new self appeared like a wraith released from Zendric's *katun*, a lamp that dispensed spirits of dead stars from far-off galaxies.

Driskoll and Kellach cried out, too, as a shower of purple fireworks exploded into geysers of amethysts.

The woodsman was gone. His simple rags pooled around his feet. His brown bushy wig and beard lay tossed aside like dead muskrats.

In his place stood a man clothed in the finest black robes encrusted with gold embroidery. It did not matter that he lacked the brawn of a woodsman. His strength was fearsome to behold.

"Nimrae," Kellach whispered.

The wizard chuckled. "Took you long enough. Zendric boasts you are his cleverest apprentice. You don't seem overly clever to me." He buffed the nails of one hand on his lapel. "But then, what does Zendric know these days? From what I hear, your wizard friend is like a puppet— "

This time Moyra had to drag Kellach back.

"How could I have been so blind?" Kellach cried. "Who else but a wizard would have the skill to fell the great tree, then sear through the trunk? Who else but *you* wanted to keep us away from the crypt?"

"And who else would tease you like a cat tossing a mouse about?" Nimrae chuckled again, clearly enjoying the moment. "And now, *Master* Kellach—" Nimrae said, gliding forward. His black eyes glittered like that magic axe blade. Moyra sensed that if Kellach didn't move, he'd be sawed in half like the tree. Or worse.

Kellach realized his danger.

"Go!" he shouted to the others. "Run!"

CHAPTER

17

Moyra took off instantly, as always. Kellach and Driskoll were close behind.

"Kell," Driskoll gasped after they had plunged into the underbrush. "What's to stop him from catching us? He can do anything!"

"Driskoll's right!" Moyra panted. "We need help! Call Moonshadow!"

"I just did," Kellach said.

Within seconds, the huge white shape materialized in the path. The wolf sat on his haunches and looked inquiringly at Kellach.

"Yes, we definitely need assistance," Kellach answered. "Nimrae—" He stopped, listening.

"He says he'll take us somewhere where Nimrae's powers can't reach." Kellach answered. He listened again. "Moonshadow says, 'Evil eyes cannot gaze into the pure eyes of the blind.'"

"What does that mean?" Driskoll asked.

But the wolf had already turned, heading through the trees. He looked back once, indicating they should follow. The kids walked for some time until Moonshadow paused in a clearing. A stream gurgled between mossy banks. An old campfire smoldered in a ring of blackened stones. Just beyond was the entrance to a cave.

"Wait!" Moyra said.

Moonshadow paused again, while Moyra lit the lantern.

"Good," Driskoll said. "I'm not afraid of the dark," he added hastily, "but I'm not wild about stumbling around in a pitch-black cave."

The kids stayed close together. The floor of the cave sometimes went downhill, sometimes tilted up. It was slow going, even with Moyra's lantern.

At last Moonshadow rounded a corner and led them into a large chamber. The small lantern barely illuminated one corner.

Along one side of the chamber, a raised rock formed a ledge, which was covered with blankets and tanned hides.

Alaric sat in the middle of the hides, legs crossed, smoking a hand-carved briarwood pipe. Moonshadow settled nearby, heaving a doglike sigh.

"Welcome to my humble abode," Alaric said, half jokingly. "I've been waiting for you."

"Alaric!" Moyra breathed. "Is this where you live?"

"How did you know we were coming?" Kellach asked.

"I heard your call for help. Remember, when one sense is taken away, others strengthen to compensate," said Alaric. "I developed extraordinary hearing and touch when I lost my sight." He patted the ledge next to him. "Please. Sit. Take food and drink. You've had a long, difficult day."

The kids collapsed in front of the fire pit. Alaric passed around a waterskin of cool spring water. They each drank deeply. Then their host gave them cakes of ground nuts studded with wild berries. The cakes tasted strange, but good.

When they had eaten their fill, Alaric said, "Moonshadow tells me Nimrae revealed himself to you."

"He tried to frighten us," Driskoll said, licking the last fragments of cake from his fingers.

"Tried!" Moyra said. "You ran like ten bugbears were on your trail. The question is, why did Nimrae reveal his true self? Why now?"

"I was wondering that very same thing," Kellach said. "Alaric, Moonshadow said that Nimrae has no power in your cave. And he can't strike down Zendric. He has to use a poppet to drain Zendric's power slowly."

Alaric nodded. "I know where you are heading, my boy. Nimrae has cracks in his armor. Hairline ones, but cracks just the same." He puffed on his pipe. "You need to find the biggest crack—where he is most vulnerable—and drive your lance into it."

Driskoll blinked. "Are we going to stab him?"

"Alaric is using an expression," Moyra explained. "Lord Dardley's fool has made fools of *us* more than once. It's time to turn the tables on him."

Kellach was gazing into the orange-blue flames of the fire. "What time is it?" he asked Alaric.

"A few minutes to curfew."

Moyra didn't ask how a blind man living in a cave could tell the difference between dark and daylight. It was obviously another of his highly developed senses.

"Soon it will be the last day," she whispered. "The anniversary of Lord Dardley's murder."

"Nimrae's army rises tomorrow night," Alaric intoned. "Go home. Sleep, if you can. You have twenty-four hours to find the crypt and save Curston."

Dejected and weary, the kids allowed Moonshadow to accompany them through the woods to the city gate.

"Meet at the obelisk at dawn," Kellach said. No more words were needed.

As Moyra walked to Broken Town, careful to avoid watchers, she did not hear voices, only her lonely footsteps echoing on the cobblestones.

CHAPTER

18

The day dawned damp and foggy. Moyra stood at her window, listening. A dog barked down the street. An owl called, returning from the night's hunt. And she heard, or thought she heard, the muted sounds of ringing steel, a screaming horse, and crying Knights who faced the creature they had thought would be their salvation.

The griffon.

Moyra remembered the engraved griffon her fingers had traced on the key, and how she'd turned the key over and touched the wheel map. The *griffon* was the key, literally, to saving Curston. If it didn't kill them first.

She had dressed in the predawn silence. Ready to face the worst danger of all, she tiptoed out of her house.

Kellach and Driskoll were at the obelisk. Kellach's face was tight with determination.

"Did you sleep?" he asked her.

"A little." Actually, she'd spent what was left of the night staring at the ceiling over her bed, thinking.

"We didn't sleep much either," Driskoll admitted.

Farmers bringing milk, eggs, and cheese trickled into the market in Main Square. Moyra wished she could tell them this might be their last day in Curston. But they would not believe her.

"I've been thinking—" Kellach began.

"Me too," Moyra said. "About the—"

The clatter of horses made them turn toward Phoenix Quarter.

"It's Lord Dardley," said Driskoll. "And Lady Caroline. Why are they here at this hour? I thought nobles slept late."

Lord Dardley's chestnut stallion cantered into the square, causing a young goatherd to jump back or be run down. Lord Dardley gave a childish giggle. He sounded, Moyra observed, like a man who had the sense of a two-year-old. How was he able to run a manor estate?

Among Lord Dardley's retinue was Nimrae. As he rode, he spied the kids. His haughty expression said he knew he would win.

Resplendent in a midnight-blue velvet riding gown, Lady Caroline rode behind him. She stared straight ahead, as if the kids didn't exist.

"What's with her?" Driskoll asked. "She acts like we're dog boys or something."

"She can't acknowledge us," Kellach said. "Or her father would wonder why. And Nimrae."

"That's right," Moyra said. "He never mentioned Lady Caroline. How does he know we are looking for the crypt? Who ratted us out? I bet it was that Mary."

"She wouldn't betray Lady Caroline," Kellach said.

Moyra wasn't so sure. Everyone seemed to be someone else.

The party rode to the center of the square and dismounted. Lord Dardley and Nimrae sampled nutmeats from a merchant just setting up. Without paying, Moyra noted with disgust.

Lady Caroline walked around with a market basket over her arm, purchasing eggs and cheese. She drifted over to where the children stood in shadow.

"Don't look at me," she said, busily arranging the items in her basket. "Tell me why you are standing here like mules! Why have you not found the crypt! At midnight tonight, Nimrae will unleash his army. And Curston will be finished!"

"We know where the crypt is," Kellach said. "We just haven't gotten to it yet, thanks to Nimrae." He explained what happened with the fallen tree.

Lady Caroline dropped a round of cheese. "No! Is this true?" A vein twitched in Lady Caroline's temple.

"Yes," Kellach said. "Nimrae is on to us. We have to distract him, keep him from following us. Can you get him out of the way?"

"Watch me." With a scream, Lady Caroline ran across the square, flinging the contents of her basket away from her. Eggs splattered everywhere.

"Father!" she shrieked. "Father! Someone has stolen my amethyst brooch!"

"What?" Lord Dardley looked dazed. "Are you sure?"

Lady Caroline clutched her throat. "Of course I'm sure! I pinned it to my cloak this morning, and now it's gone!"

"That's terrible," said Lord Dardley. He turned to Nimrae. "What should we do?"

The wizard turned up his palms to the sky. "Perhaps Lady Caroline is mistaken. Perhaps the brooch is in her jewelry casket at home."

"Good thinking," said Lord Dardley. "We'll go back—"

"No!" Lady Caroline's sharp voice made both men step back. "I want every man to look for my brooch. You, father, are going to get Torin. The watch needs to be involved. And Nimrae, you lead the search. Every inch of Main Square. We're not leaving here until you find my brooch!"

"I just hope Lady Caroline can keep up that act," Kellach said.

"She's good," Moyra said. "Let's hurry before Nimrae tries to search us too."

CHAPTER

19

The kids zipped through the square, out of the Oldgate, and all the way back to Dardley Hall. Soon they were back at the game preserve.

Kellach pushed them at a furious pace, checking for the *K*s he'd slashed on trees that indicated the trails that did not lead to the center of the forest.

"This way!" he panted when he found the tree without the mark.

They ran like demons down the narrow path until they reached the enormous tree Nimrae had felled across their path like a piece of straw.

"I bet he closed up the opening," Driskoll said.

He was right. The trunk wasn't even seared, much less sliced in two.

Kellach threw his pack on the ground. "Moyra, get out your rope. Hurry!"

"My rope isn't long enough to reach over this huge trunk," Moyra said. "And we only have two."

Kellach ignored her. He cut his own rope and gave half to Driskoll. "Get ready to climb!"

He muttered the magic word. The ropes stiffened.

"Up!" Kellach ordered. The ropes responded, lifting into the air.

To the others, Kellach added, "The ropes can only elevate a few feet at a time. Hang on tight!"

Gripping their ropes, the three kids rose over the enormous tree as Kellach yelled, "Up! Up!" When they stood on top of the trunk, he reversed the spell, and the ropes lowered them slowly to the other side.

They hit the ground running, their feet fueled by the knowledge that the crypt was at the end of the path. They ran and ran. Pain shredded Moyra's lungs, but she didn't stop. She wondered if the path would ever end.

At last the forest gave way to a clearing. The path looped around in a circle. In its center was a mound covered with tender grass the color of eternal spring.

"That's it!" Moyra exclaimed.

"That's the crypt?" Driskoll asked. "Looks more like a hill to me."

Kellach closed his eyes in concentration. "There's a door inside!"

"Do we have to dig up all that grass?" Driskoll asked.

"I left my spade at home."

"No." Kellach cracked his knuckles. Then he made funny motions, like an old woman knitting. "I just learned this spell. I hope it works."

As Kellach's hands worked the knitting motion, the grass peeled back. Next, layers of dirt and rock stripped away. The mound whittled away until finally all that was left was a square slab of stone.

The kids slowly approached, half afraid of what they might find.

Kellach brushed loose dirt and pebbles from the surface, revealing the outline of a griffon carved into a granite slab. He took the key from his pouch.

The griffons were identical.

CHAPTER

20

A sickle-shaped moon shared the early morning sky with the sun. In the long grass, small creatures were stirring. All the animals—and strange beings—that shunned the light of day were creeping back to their holes and dens.

Spooky laughter echoed beyond the trees.

"Doesn't the griffon guard the crypt?" Moyra asked uneasily. "Where is it?"

Kellach looked around. "I don't see any sign of it. No big bed or whatever a griffon would sleep in."

"I can't believe the griffon would just let us walk right into the crypt," Driskoll said. "Not with its nasty temper."

"We can't worry about that now," Kellach told him. "We've got to hurry."

The kids stood nervously by the shadow-swathed crypt. Kellach twisted the silver key in his hand.

"Where's the lock?" Driskoll said.

Kellach searched beneath the crevice below the lid. "Here." He pointed to a mossy disk, then scraped it with his knife to reveal the keyhole. A ghostly cloud temporarily veiled the morning sun. Kellach looked up.

"Don't look!" Moyra shivered even though it wasn't chilly. "It's bad luck to view the moon through tree branches. My granny used to say so."

"What could be worse than having Curston destroyed?" Kellach said. "It's weird to see the moon and the sun in the same sky, though."

He checked the sky again. The empty eye socket of the moon sliver glared balefully down at them. The topmost branches of the tallest tree seemed to snag the moon with their bone-colored tips.

Over the crypt, a shadow took flight like a large, predatory bird taking wing. Moyra glanced up. *Was* that a bird? She thought she saw broad wings and the long tail of a hawk.

The lock glimmered, waiting for the key. Kellach's hand shook as he inserted it into the lock.

"It fits," he said.

"How are we supposed to lift the lid?" Driskoll asked. "It must weigh more than the bells of St. Cuthbert's—"

By itself, the lid slid sideways, revealing a dark hole in the ground. Instantly a ghastly smell seeped upward in a noxious yellow vapor. The odor went straight down into the pits of their stomachs.

"Blech." Driskoll gagged.

Moyra wiped her streaming eyes. "What did you expect? A crypt would smell like a bouquet of violets?"

"Be quiet, you two," Kellach said. "We've got to find the Knights and wake them. Somehow."

They stepped up to the entrance to the crypt, balancing on the granite slab, and looked inside. The sun chose that moment to hide behind another passing cloud. Moyra teetered on the slab, nearly tumbling over the ledge.

Then the cloud drifted, allowing sunlight to illuminate part of the inside. The rest remained draped in darkness. Moss-slick steps led downward into blackness.

"*Luminere*," Kellach said. He held up his knife like a torch. It glowed from pommel to tip as if it burned from within.

Even with the knife's light, the darkness swallowed the scuffings of their boots as they descended the slippery steps, their hammering heartbeats, and even the stale air. By the time they had half-slid to the bottom, they were all breathing hard.

"Where do you think the Knights are?" Driskoll whispered, staying close to his brother.

Kellach waved his flickering light. There were two doors, one on each side of the corridor. "Looks like there are two chambers."

"What do you bet the doors are locked?" Moyra said. "Anything to slow us down."

"Look!" Driskoll said, awestruck.

The right-hand door began to glow. Red lines appeared on the door, forming a shape.

"It's a shield!" said Kellach. "With a dragon in the shape of an S . . . The symbol of the Knights! They must be in here." He reached for the engraved knob, and gave a small push. The door swung open.

Come in.

The words weren't exactly spoken. More like sighed.

"Who said that?" Moyra said.

"I thought it was you, making a joke," said Driskoll.

She frowned at him. "Who would make a joke in a place like this?"

"Be quiet!" Kellach warned them again. They crept into the musty chamber.

Nine lifeless figures rested upon marble biers. They lay on their backs, their swords placed decorously across their bodies. At their feet, shields were propped against the biers. Cobwebs swagged from helmets to boots. A layer of choking thick dust covered the silent warriors, giving them a chalky appearance.

The kids walked warily among the biers, trailing cobwebs until they, too, looked like wraiths. Whispered voices, murmurs of anguish, wove patterns around them.

"They look like they'll crumble if you touch them," Driskoll said.

"I'm not planning on touching them," Moyra said.

"We have to," said Kellach grimly. "We have to wake them

up. And get them ready to fight by midnight."

Moyra heaved a sigh. "It might take us all day to figure out how to get them up."

Kellach held up his hands and grinned. "Relax. I've got it covered. Just watch this." In the feeble glow of the light from his knife, Kellach began chanting, twisting his fingers in the air.

Moyra stared at the lifeless Knights. Nothing happened.

Kellach cleared his throat. "Not a problem. I've got another even better idea." He muttered something under his breath and again traced a strange pattern in the air.

Still . . . nothing.

He tried spell after spell. Nothing worked.

At last, he closed his eyes. "Maybe an idea will come to me." After a moment, he opened them again. The Knights were still dead.

"Oh, for Cuthbert's sake!" Moyra said. "Get up!"

One by one, the spirits of the deceased sat up, like sleepy figures sitting up in bed, leaving their useless bodies lying flat. The movements of their rising made a soft feathery rustle.

Driskoll's mouth dropped open. "All you had to do was say the obvious!"

"Well, genius," Kellach said to Moyra. "They're awake. What next?"

"I'm not sure," she replied. "It seems kind of rude to tell them to go fight another ghost army."

"They look kind of flimsy anyway," Driskoll said. "Like a

good wind would blow them over. *Can* they fight?"

Kellach approached the first bier. The Knight looked through him but seemed alert. Kellach cleared his throat importantly. "Um-*hum*. Uh—who were you in your previous life?"

The ghost Knight's lips barely stirred. "Agilard."

"Nice to meet you, Agilard. I'm Kellach. One of the new Knights of the Silver Dragon."

Agilard nodded. He was a handsome warrior, with strong, capable features. He held a dusty silver sword in one hand. In his other hand, he carried a Silver Dragon shield.

Kellach moved down the biers, asking each ghost his name in turn.

"Baldric," came the answer from a roguish man with a close-cut goatee and a red headband tied around his forehead.

"Alenna," said a thin elvish figure in a flowing blue robe.

Moyra was glad to see a female Knight among the ranks.

When all the Knights had identified themselves, their bodies joined their wavering spirits. They sheathed their swords and climbed down off the biers. They stood at attention, holding their helmets under one arm.

Moyra nudged Kellach in the ribs. "I think they're waiting for you to give them an order."

"Upstairs!" he commanded the Knights.

With squeaks and clanks, the Knights marched single file out of the chamber and up the steps. The kids followed, glad to be out of the tomb.

The forest beyond the crypt was ominously silent. The Knights gathered in the grassy clearing nearby.

Kellach looked around. "I guess we should give the Knights some exercises. They look a little rusty."

Driskoll stood in front of the Knights, pointed to himself, then touched his toes. The Knights followed suit.

Moyra thought the Knights looked bewildered, like children awakened in the middle of a dream.

"This is ridiculous!" she scoffed. "How will touching their toes help them fight Nimrae's ghost army!"

Kellach narrowed his eyes. "If you have an idea about how to train them to fight, you're more than welcome to go ahead."

"I just mean . . . we need someone who knows something about warfare to train them! Someone who has had experience in battle—"

A vision in white drifted into the clearing. The kids tensed. Another ghost?

Wearing snowy robes, Alaric hurried into the clearing, using his sword as a cane. "Children! I sensed that you had opened the tomb!"

Moyra grinned. "Alaric! You're right on time." Moyra looked behind him searching for his giant companion. "But . . . how did you get here without Moonshadow? He's all right, isn't he?"

Alaric nodded. "Moonshadow is tracking the griffon. My wolf pointed me in the right direction, but I had to make my way here alone."

"I hope Moonshadow will be all right," said Driskoll. "But at least we won't have to worry about the griffon coming back for a nap in its lair."

Emotion broke over Alaric's features. "Oh! My comrades! They will listen to me."

Alaric divided the knights into two groups. The two groups parried and thrust their swords as they mock-fought. Moyra, Kellach, and Driskoll fetched dropped shields and swords.

"They're not very good, are they?" Driskoll said to Moyra.

"Nimrae's army is going to whip the Knights," she predicted direly. "Maybe they'll shape up in another few hours."

"Alaric," Kellach said, watching a Knight trip over a root. "Do you really think our side can win?"

"These men faced bitter defeat ten years ago," said Alaric. "They will relish the opportunity to prove their worth again."

Just then a hunting horn sounded in the woods. *Ah-roooo! Ah-rooo!*

"Lord Dardley?" Moyra asked. "He wouldn't be hunting today!"

"It is not Lord Dardley." Alaric sounded grim. "It's Nimrae's army."

"Nimrae's army!" Driskoll exclaimed. "They're coming *here*. But how did they know we'd raised the Knights?"

Moyra caught a glimpse of darkness taking flight over the crypt. "Nimrae's goshawk was spying on us. I thought I saw it a little while ago." She flapped her arms in imitation of a huge bird. "It told its master we found the crypt."

"And Nimrae must have ordered his men to demolish us before destroying Curston," Kellach added.

Moyra felt as if an icy hand encircled her neck. Nimrae's fearsome army was here . . . and they were not ready.

Daylight disappeared like a snuffed lantern. It was as black as night.

Moyra gasped.

"What happened?" Kellach asked.

Alaric's voice sounded bitter. "Nimrae meant to fight at midnight. But you raised the Knights early, so he has raised his own army and called darkness back. That way he can have the advantage."

"In other words," Driskoll said, "he cheated."

Thrump, thrump. The steady beat of marching feet drummed toward them.

"They're awfully noisy for ghosts," Driskoll observed. "Maybe Nimrae got real people instead. If that's true, we've got a chance. When the real people see our ghost Knights, they'll run away."

"Nimrae's army is as dead as winter," said Alaric. "Have no fear."

But Moyra *was* afraid and grew more so as the pounding feet drew closer. The woods shook with the heavy rattle of lances, swords, and armor. Then, in a burst of purple fireworks, the enemy made a mighty appearance. Foot soldiers stood shoulder to shoulder, lance to lance, shield to shield. Hundreds of them, it seemed.

In a shower of fiery sparks, Nimrae himself led the army, riding on a midnight black stallion. The wind blew the purple plume on his helmet. Instead of body armor, he wore a purple tunic.

"So the crypt *is* really here," Nimrae said, sounding delighted. "And all along I thought it was somewhere beneath Curston. Oh, well. I'll destroy the city anyway. Build myself a brand-new one, with slave labor."

As he laughed, the fireworks fizzled out and all was dark again.

"What is he talking about?" Kellach asked Moyra. "Why did he want to find the crypt?"

"Ready to be defeated a *second* time, Blind Knight?" Nimrae taunted from the darkness.

Unable to ride at the head of his army, Alaric commanded from the edge of the crypt.

"Comrades! For Curston and your honor!" he bellowed. "Charge!"

The Knights of the Silver Dragon surged forth to meet Nimrae's army. Swords clanged. Men and women cried out. The Knights stumbled and wandered like moles in the forest.

"They act like they can't see!" Moyra said.

"Maybe they can't," Driskoll said.

"Our army needs light, Kell," Moyra said. "Can you help!"

"*Luminere!*" he muttered, concentrating. The veins in his head pulsed with the effort. "*Luminere! Luminere!*" He chanted feverishly.

A lit candle appeared on a tree branch. Then two.

Kellach leaned against a tree. "My head is killing me. I'm not used to concentrating so hard."

But he kept on chanting. The next tree began sprouting candles too, and the next. Soon the forest was bright as midday.

"It's a miracle!" Moyra exclaimed.

But the light didn't stop there. A candle glowed above Agilard, then above Alenna and Faxon and Baldric, until all the knights had a candle lighting their way. No matter how strongly the wind blew, the candles did not flicker.

"Good work, Kell," Moyra said.

Kellach's knees buckled, and he collapsed at Moyra's feet.

CHAPTER

21

Moyra knelt instantly. "Kell! Are you all right?"

Driskoll rushed to his brother's side. "He's exhausted from doing all that magic." He shook Kellach's arm. "Kell!"

"Let me sleep . . ." Kellach mumbled.

"You can't rest yet." Moyra hauled him to his feet. "The Knights have to win, or all your hard work will be for nothing."

The Knights leaped into the fray, swinging swords and fists. They seemed heartened by the presence of light, as if the golden glow symbolized their cause. They fought fiercely, determined to undo an old wrong and vanquish evil.

But for all their energy, the Knights were woefully outnumbered. Foot soldiers kept marching from the forest, three abreast.

From his horse, Nimrae cackled with delight. "Give it to 'em, boys!" he cried, swinging his sword over his head. "We still have a city to conquer!" His black eyes sparkled with the anticipation of victory.

Agilard, the burliest Knight, whacked the flat of his sword on an enemy's helmet. The man thrust his own sword into Agilard's visor. Agilard screamed in agony and fell to his knees. Nimrae's soldier tossed back his own visor and spit contemptuously on the hapless man.

Horrified, Moyra saw that Nimrae's soldier did not have a face, only two blank eyeholes and another hole for his mouth. The soldier put his helmet back on, but not before turning his empty gaze on Moyra. The mouth hole formed a grin, like someone grimacing in death.

She whirled around to Kellach, who was still holding his aching head.

"I know you're wiped out from all the magic," she said. "But we've got to do something." She pointed at three Knights lying on the ground. "The Knights of the Silver Dragon are dropping like flies. We can't just sit here!"

"I don't have the strength to put on armor and fight," he said. "You and Dris go ahead."

"Not us." Moyra glanced back at Alaric, who stood by the battle with a worried expression on his face. "Alaric. He's our last hope."

"But he can't see," said Driskoll. "We don't want him to get hurt either. Or possibly killed."

Moyra stared at the elderly Knight, who was barking orders

to his troops. "Somehow, I think this is more his fight than anyone's."

"Are you crazy?" Driskoll said. "We're trying to save an entire city!"

"I know," Moyra agreed. "But battles are won by individuals fighting for a cause. Don't Knights live by a code of honor? I believe Alaric desperately needs to regain his honor."

Kellach nodded. "Makes sense to me. Alaric may be able to rally the Knights if he leads them personally. Let's see what he says."

Alaric leaped at the idea.

"I don't need my eyes," he said. "Fighting flows through my veins. My feet know where to take me. My arm still has the strength to heft a sword. My nose will tell me which man is my enemy—"

"You can smell Nimrae's soldiers?" Driskoll asked.

Alaric nodded. "They stink of rot and death and nameless things best left buried where they came from. I only need an article from a fair lady to bring me luck." He reached his hand out to Moyra.

Moyra blushed. "You mean somebody like Lady Caroline, not me—" But she took the vellum envelope with the four-leaf clover she had received from Rom and gave it to Alaric.

"Now I'm ready." He plummeted into the thick of the fight with a bloodcurdling yell.

At first Nimrae's soldiers fell back at the sight of the warrior tearing toward them. A mutter rippled through the enemy like a tiger running through the jungle.

"The Blind Knight!"

"He's only a pitiful old man!" Nimrae screamed at his army. "Form ranks! Charge!"

"Charge!" Alaric called to the Knights.

He streaked into the middle of Nimrae's soldiers, slashing right and left with his sword. Moyra admired the blind man's bravery and skill. Amid the clamor and noise, Alaric almost seemed to rise above the battle, and yet every dig and thrust he made was with deadly accuracy. She could only imagine what a great Knight he had been before he lost his sight.

But Nimrae's troops pushed the Knights of the Silver Dragon deeper into the tangled forest. In the confusion, it would be harder to fight. Despite Alaric's rallying cries, the Knights were flagging.

Amazingly, the darkness became tinged with faint gray.

"Look!" Moyra said, pointing to the sky.

"Daylight. It's just beyond Nimrae's false night," said Kellach.

"What will happen when day comes back?" she asked.

"Maybe the daylight will break through," Driskoll said hopefully. "Then Nimrae won't have time to destroy Curston."

Kellach shook his head. "He's not that dumb."

As if on cue, Nimrae galloped to the front lines. "Fall back!"

he bawled. "Leave these scoundrels. They are too weak to hurt a flea. On to Curston!"

He stood in his stirrups and raised his gloved fist. A huge bird swooped down from the treetops and settled on its master's fist.

Nimrae is in full power, Moyra thought. Nothing can stop him now.

Kellach must have read her mind, because he stated, "It's not over yet. We still have one trick up our sleeve . . ."

"What?" Driskoll watched one of the enemy swat Faxon to the ground like a mosquito.

"The griffon."

Moyra and Driskoll both stared at him.

"You can't mean—" Moyra said, incredulous.

"Deliberately bring that beast here?" Driskoll looked stunned.

Kellach's mind was set. "We have no choice."

"How are you going to get him here?" asked Moyra.

"The griffon hates me the most. I teased it with the horse and then made the horse disappear," Kellach replied. "It'll be only too glad to come finish me off."

He headed in the direction where Alaric had said Moonshadow was tracking the beast.

"Wait!" Driskoll pulled him back. "You'll be killed, and we'll still lose the battle. What will that accomplish?"

"Alaric said griffons can sometimes work for justice,"

Kellach said. "Perhaps I can convince it to fight for us."

"When Dardley tried to use the griffon to fight for good, he failed!" Driskoll tugged on his robes. "Don't go, Kellach."

Kellach gently plucked Driskoll's hand from his sleeve. "I have to do this, Dris. I'm the only one."

Moyra pulled Driskoll back. "So many people are counting on us. We have to let him go."

She turned to Kellach. "Be careful. And remember you have Rom's coral, the magic stone from the sea."

Kellach gave her a weak smile. "I'll need it."

Then he disappeared into the forest.

CHAPTER

22

Alaric trotted up and flung back the visor of his helmet. "Where is Kellach?"

"He—he went to lure the griffon," Moyra admitted.

Alaric nodded once. "Indeed. The young wizard is very brave. The only reason I haven't been griffon bait myself is Moonshadow's protection."

"You said that the griffon once fought for good," Moyra reminded him. "Do you think this one will again?"

Alaric gazed into the woods with his sightless eyes. "That remains to be seen. Well, I'd better rally what troops I have left."

Meanwhile, Nimrae had reorganized his own army. His soldiers were marching away from the battle, with the exception of a few that were still engaged in swordplay with the Knights.

"Bye-bye!" Nimrae called to Alaric. "See you around!" He laughed at his own joke and cantered after his army, purple plume bobbing.

"There goes Curston," Driskoll said dismally.

Alaric sagged, his shoulders bowed in defeat. "I failed again! I don't deserve the title 'Knight.'"

"You did the best you could," said Moyra. "It's not your fault Nimrae's army was bigger than ours."

"I didn't deserve a second chance—" Alaric's words were cut off by a high-pitched scream.

Moyra's heart stalled. She knew that cry.

"The griffon!" Driskoll exclaimed. "It's coming! Where is Kellach? I hope he got away!"

The beast flew into the clearing with powerful wingbeats and landed mere feet from them.

Alaric quickly positioned himself between the kids and the griffon. The griffon unsheathed its deadly claws, but Alaric stood his ground.

The griffon roared in Alaric's direction.

"You were on our side once!" Alaric shouted back. "In the name of all that is right, fight with us again! To honor those brave men whose souls you guard."

The griffon actually seemed to be considering. Moyra was astonished.

"Go!" Alaric commanded the griffon. "Stop them from reaching the city!"

The griffon soared away. Nimrae's army hadn't yet left the clearing—his invincible ghost warriors were slowing down. Nimrae had doubled back through the ranks to speed them along. His eyes widened when the griffon landed in front of his black stallion. The goshawk flapped away, deserting its master.

The griffon snapped its beak.

The black horse bucked Nimrae off and galloped madly into the forest. Nimrae struggled to his feet, helmet askew. He tore it off and stared angrily at the kids.

"You fools! Do you know what you've done! I almost had it! Now no one will *ever* get it!"

"What is he babbling about?" Driskoll asked. "Almost had what?"

Nimrae started running, but the griffon reached out one foot, snagged the wizard's purple tunic, and reeled him back. Nimrae screamed as the griffon pinned him down with its wicked claws.

"Like a cat with a mouse," Moyra remarked.

Driskoll pointed up at the sky. "Look!"

The grayish tinge in the sky was now an orange-pink light. The light grew stronger until the woods were bathed in warm daylight.

Like water thrown on flames, Nimrae's ghost army began to fade. Suits of armor collapsed in clanking ranks until the ground seemed littered with life-sized tin dolls.

"Unbelievable!" Moyra breathed.

The Knights lined up and began filing back into the yawning crypt.

Alaric waved. "Farewell, comrades."

Driskoll turned to the griffon, which still had Nimrae trapped. "Where is my brother? What did you do with him?"

"Nothing," said a familiar voice.

Kellach rode into the clearing on Moonshadow's back. The white wolf stopped and let Kellach slide off his back.

Moyra and Driskoll ran over.

"Are you okay?" Driskoll demanded.

"Not a scratch on me, as you can see." He patted Moonshadow. "Moonshadow protected me. Then I ran this way until the griffon caught the scent of a horse and a bigger prize." He indicated Nimrae. "How does it feel to be the mouse for a change?"

"Only Zendric's apprentice would be a bigger fool than he is!" the wizard spat.

"He keeps rambling about almost having something," Moyra said. "We can't make sense of it."

"If we have permission." Kellach faced the griffon, brows raised in question.

The griffon nodded.

"That's very gracious of you," said Kellach. "And thank you for coming back to our side."

Moyra's head spun like the Wheel of Fortune. She had no idea what Kellach was talking about.

"This way." Kellach grabbed one of the remaining candles and descended into the crypt.

Driskoll followed him, then Alaric, with Moyra bringing up the rear. She watched to make sure the blind Knight would not trip. But his boots found each stone tread as surely as if he had chiseled the granite himself.

At the bottom, they stood before the two doors. The door marked with the Silver Dragon shield was firmly closed. The Knights were slumbering once more, on their cobweb-draped biers, clasping their swords.

But Alaric approached the other door. The doorknob he twisted was plain brass. No carving appeared as it had on the Knights' door.

Just then Moyra realized what was inside. Now she knew what Nimrae had truly wanted.

The door squeaked open and they all stepped inside.

CHAPTER

23

The high-ceilinged chamber glowed like a thousand suns. Gold chalices, vases, and goblets covered gold-leafed tables. Golden swords and shields leaned against the stone walls. Gold statues of people and animals vied for space with gold trunks and jewel boxes. Heavy gold link necklaces, wristlets, arm cuffs, cloak brooches, and ornate rings spilled out of carved gold caskets.

On every surface—tables, chairs, and the floor—mountains of gold coins spoke of long, dangerous journeys to distant lands. Tiny finials from the Isle of Dreama, cupped coins unearthed from Sharian tombs, Sassanian gold shells, square coins struck by goldsmiths from Parthia.

In the middle of the room, gleaming nuggets formed a hollowed bowl that looked like a giant bird's nest. An enormous egg-shaped, blue-veined rock was cradled in the center.

"The griffon's lair!" Moyra said, dazzled. "This is what it guards!"

"She," Kellach corrected. "That's her egg."

Alaric nodded. "It's made of agate. She only lays one egg every five hundred years. Agate has magic properties. It is supposed to make you invisible and protect you from danger."

"With a chunk of agate that big, you could be invisible forever. Where did the rest of this stuff come from? Does it all belong to the griffon?" Driskoll stroked a gold sword hilt studded with rubies and emeralds.

"No, the rest of this is ours," Kellach said.

Driskoll's jaw dropped. "You mean, we can have it?" He started to pick up the jeweled sword.

"No, I mean all this gold belongs to our town. It's the Lost Gold of Curston."

"Someone had the foresight to move the treasure before the Sundering," Alaric added. "Here, it is safe."

"But we can't use it!" Driskoll protested. "What good is gold if we can't spend it?"

"What good, indeed?" said an authoritative voice from the doorway.

The kids whirled. A tall, stately man strode into the treasure room in a swirl of scarlet velvet, followed by Lady Caroline.

Lady Caroline beamed with happiness.

"Lord Dardley!" said Kellach. "What are you doing here?"

"Checking to see if you three are all right." Lord Dardley's expression was stern and serious, a vast change from his bewildered manner.

"What about you?" Moyra asked Lady Caroline.

Lady Caroline rushed forward to clasp Moyra's hands. "I'm wonderful! And so is my father. He's well again!"

Moyra smiled. "When did you get here?"

"I tried to hold Nimrae off for as long as possible," Lady Caroline began, "but Nimrae saw through my charade not long after you three left Main Square. He rode off, claiming he had to see to an experiment back at the manor. I knew he was lying, of course, but what more could I do? Father insisted on riding into the forest after him. I tried to delay him because—well, I didn't know what would happen. We got here just as the griffon cornered Nimrae. And with Nimrae's capture, that cloud that's covered Father's face for weeks suddenly passed. He's his old self. I can't thank you enough!"

Lord Dardley put his arm around his daughter's shoulders. "My mind feels strong and sharp. I will never let anyone poison it again." His gaze rested on Alaric, who had been standing by quietly. "May I have the pleasure of your name, sir?"

The Knight knelt before Lord Dardley. "Sir Alaric, former Knight of the Silver Dragon, at your service, m'lord. I was—with your father in the Troll Invasion."

"Rise, Sir Alaric," said the nobleman. "I am honored to meet the only survivor of the battle that claimed my father. Please accept my hospitality."

"Very kind of you, sir. I don't want to be a burden—" Alaric began, but Lord Dardley cut him off.

"Nonsense. You can teach my young guards how to fight."
Lord Dardley looked at the kids. "I suspect you three can teach them a thing or two yourselves. We'd better vacate this chamber. The griffon is probably restless. I'm surprised she has trusted us around her egg this long."

When they were all out of the crypt, the lid slid sideways again until the hole was covered. Kellach started to lock it with the silver key, but Lord Dardley held out his hand.

"That belongs to me, I believe."

Kellach gave him the key. "I'm glad to be rid of it."

Moyra stared at the griffon and Nimrae. The griffon hadn't moved a claw. Nimrae was still pinned inside the pearly razor cage. Four of Lord Dardley's guards stood a respectful distance away, their lances leveled at Nimrae.

"Kellach," Lord Dardley said. "What shall we do with this sorry excuse of a wizard? Kill him? Exile him? Let our griffon eat him for dinner?"

"Can the griffon fly with him?" Kellach asked.

Alaric nodded. "According to legend, Alexander the Great tried to ride a griffon to the edge of the sky. He thought he could do anything, but arrogant pride was his downfall."

"I can't think of anyone more arrogant than Nimrae," said Lady Caroline. "I vote we let the griffon carry *him* to the edge of the sky."

"Me too," Driskoll said.

"No!" yelled Nimrae. "Give me another chance!"

Lord Dardley ignored him. "Wise decision, daughter. Is it unanimous?"

After six *yea's* were counted, Lord Dardley issued the order. "Carry him far from Dardley Hall, far from Curston, as far as you can. If you drop him, no one will be heartbroken."

"Take him away!" Alaric commanded.

The griffon unfurled her wings, clutched Nimrae in a firmer grip, and prepared to take flight.

Alaric stepped closer. "Thank you again for coming back to our side."

The griffon nodded and took off heavily. Nimrae screamed and flailed his legs, but to no avail. The griffon soared over the treetops, and Nimrae's cries died away.

24

L ady Caroline motioned for one of the guards. "Lend your horses to these brave Knights and Alaric. You guards can walk back to Dardley Hall."

When everyone was mounted, they began the trek through the game preserve. The woods, which had seemed so threatening before, rang with birdsong.

Lord Dardley led the group on his chestnut stallion. Moyra rode behind him on a white horse with a dark brown mane. As they cantered through the forest, she couldn't help but wonder about everything that had come to pass. "There's still one thing I don't understand, Lord Dardley. Why did you build this crypt way out here in the middle of the game preserve for the Knights of the Silver Dragon?"

"I didn't build the crypt, my father did," Lord Dardley explained. "He was charged by the Knights of the Silver Dragon with protecting Curston's treasure. He had this structure built at the very center of the game preserve as a safe haven for securing Curston's gold."

"Good thing he did," Moyra said. "In the Sundering, Curston's own treasury burned to the ground."

"Do you think the Knights of the Silver Dragon anticipated the Sundering?" Kellach asked.

"I'm not sure," answered Lord Dardley. "Father was asked to guard the treasure long before the Sundering. I know that strange forces had been about in the land for some time, stirring up trouble, and pitting one group against another. These forces inspired the trolls to invade my father's land. I was gone on a quest of my own when the battle occurred. By the time I came home, he was already buried in the Dardley ancestral cemetery. For a long time I was grief-stricken. I blamed the Knights of the Silver Dragon for my father's death. I felt they should have protected him. So I had the Knights from that battle laid to rest in the structure Father built to store Curston's gold. I did not want to return their bodies to Curston, where they would be praised as martyrs. But . . . now I realize how selfish I'd been. I was wrong."

Alaric squeezed his reins tightly.

Moyra leaned across her saddle. "It's over now," she said softly.

"Where does the griffon come in?" Driskoll asked.

"Father originally brought the griffon to Dardley Hall to protect Curston's treasure," Lord Dardley replied. "He knew that griffons guard gold. As long as no one bothered her, she left people alone. She did so well guarding the treasure that Father got the bright idea to train the griffon to serve him in battle as well. Of course . . . that's when things went terribly wrong."

Lady Caroline frowned. "And then things got worse when Nimrae came and poisoned your mind."

Lord Dardley nodded. "I liked the idea of having a house wizard. It never dawned on me that Nimrae would work for evil. Stupid of me, of course. I suppose he wormed himself into my mind from the moment I met him."

They picked up the main path leading to Dardley Hall.

"What was Nimrae really after?" Kellach asked. "Did he want to destroy Curston? Or did he want the gold in the crypt? Or the agate egg? Didn't he have enough power?"

"He wanted it all," replied Lord Dardley. "His greed knew no boundaries. I didn't realize it when he took over my mind, but I am certain he planned to convert Curston into a slave colony while draping himself in all its riches. He could conjure a ghost army, but he could not make gold. No wizard can."

"Zendric's been working on the philosopher's stone for ages," Driskoll put in. "It's supposed to turn metals into gold. Zendric says it won't ever work, but he likes tinkering with it."

"Zendric!" Moyra, Kellach, and Driskoll exclaimed at the same time. They looked at each other.

"I explained to my father what Nimrae has done to Zendric," said Lady Caroline.

They came around a bend, within sight of the door in the wall.

"Nimrae's plan to destroy Curston failed, but the poppet is still in Zendric's house," Kellach cried. "He may be dead by now!"

"Go," Lord Dardley said. "Take the horses and go as fast as you can. Perhaps it won't be too late."

CHAPTER

25

At Zendric's house, Kellach nearly ripped the door off its hinges in his haste to get inside. Moyra and Driskoll were right behind him.

Zendric's room looked like it had been struck by a tornado. Robes, hats, beakers, books, pillows, and more were strewn all over the floor.

Two men stood in front of Zendric's armchair. They wheeled around when they heard the kids.

"Dad!" Moyra cried. "Rom! What are you two doing here?" She didn't know who she was more surprised to see.

Rom tipped his hat back. "Your father brought me here, Chavi. He told me the wizard was worse, and I came to help."

Kellach turned to Moyra. "Did you tell your father about Zendric? About any of what we were doing?"

"Moyra is loyal to the core," Breddo said defensively. "I

keep an ear to the ground. Working at Dardley Hall, I heard things. Saw things."

"I saw you the time Wat pretended to be sick!" Moyra said.

"Yes," said her father. "There was a lot of dramatizing going on. I heard your name come up, along with Kellach's and Driskoll's, once when Lady Caroline was talking to Wat. I figured you were involved in dangerous business. I hung around to keep an eye on you."

"So that's why you didn't come home after the hunt?" Moyra asked.

Breddo nodded. "I took his Lordship's huntsmen to the Skinned Cat. They talk more when they are deep in their cups." Her father looked at her. "Don't you trust your old man?"

A wheezy rattle snapped their attention to Zendric's armchair. The wizard sat still, eyes closed, fragile as a just-hatched sparrow. His breathing was shallow and raspy.

"Breddo heard Lady Caroline tell Wat about the poppet and Zendric being bad off," Rom filled in. "Since you were trying to save Curston, Breddo and me came to save Zendric."

"But we can't find that poppet thing anywhere," Breddo said sadly.

"We've looked too," Driskoll said. "And so has Zendric, when he was able." He began riffling through papers on a table.

"We've looked everywhere down here," Rom said.

Moyra grabbed Kellach's arm. "We can't let Nimrae destroy him!"

Kellach leaned down to Zendric. He held the wizard's thin, papery hand. "Zendric," he whispered. "Can you tell us what to do? Can anyone else help you?"

Zendric's eyes fluttered. He spoke one word, so faint Moyra wasn't sure she heard correctly.

Kellach looked at her. "What did he say?"

"He said 'staff.'"

"Staff? He must be delirious again. He's too ill to get up and walk around."

Moyra stared into space. He knew she loved his staffs. The mahogany one with the moon carved into it, the eagle-claw knobbed staff, and—Moyra's favorite—the rowan oak with a carved reddish stone that Zendric said resembled her features.

Moyra stared at the staffs stabbed into the earthen jar. The reddish stone was carved into a face, but the features looked nothing like a girl's. Instead, the carving looked remarkably like Zendric.

"I found it!" she yelled. "That's the poppet!"

Kellach saw it too and leaped at the staff. "Mary said it was made in the person's image. The stone does look like Zendric if you squint your eyes just right."

"What are you going to do with it?" Driskoll asked. "Zendric won't get better until it's destroyed."

"I'll destroy it," said Rom. "You know you can trust me."

Rom took the staff in one hand. He pointed the end with the reddish stone toward the hard floor and slammed his giant foot down upon it. With a crack, the staff broke in two, and the stone went skittering across the floor. Rom stomped on it one more time. The stone shattered into hundreds of tiny pieces.

Within minutes, Zendric opened his eyes. Color seeped back into his sunken cheeks. He flexed his fingers, then pushed himself to a sitting position. His gaze swept Kellach, Moyra, and Driskoll.

"Thank you," said Zendric. "I knew you would come through for me. And for Curston."

"There were times when we didn't think we would," Driskoll confessed.

"But we didn't give up," said Moyra.

"That is why I entrust you all with such difficult tasks," said Zendric.

"They're good kids," Breddo said. "These three."

Zendric smiled. "I know." His voice strengthened. "Kellach, you've been goofing off a lot these days. Lessons tomorrow."

Kellach grinned. "Anything you say."

Moyra left with her father. They walked through the Wizards' Quarter. When they passed the shop with the star-and-moon hat in the window, Moyra decided she didn't need it after all.

Nimrae was right about one thing. He didn't control her fortune with the spin of a wheel. She alone was responsible for her happiness or unhappiness. No matter what her father did, she would still be his daughter. And that was enough.

She slid her hand in his, and they strolled back to Broken Town, together.

MORE ADVENTURES
FOR THE

FIGURE IN THE FROST

A cold snap hits Curston and a mysterious stranger holds the key to the town's survival. But first he wants something…from Moyra. Will Moyra sacrifice her secret to save the town?

DAGGER OF DOOM

When Kellach discovers a dagger of doom with his own name burned in the blade, it seems certain someone wants him dead. But who?

THE HIDDEN DRAGON

The Knights must find the silver dragon who gave their order its name. Can they make it to the dragon's lair alive?

Ask for KNIGHTS OF THE SILVER DRAGON books at your favorite bookstore!

For ages eight to twelve

For more information visit www.mirrorstonebooks.com

EXPLORE THE MYSTERIES OF CURSTON WITH KELLACH, DRISKOLL AND MOYRA

THE SILVER SPELL

Kellach and Driskoll's mother, missing for five years, miraculously comes home. Is it a dream come true? Or is it a nightmare?

KEY TO THE GRIFFON'S LAIR

Will the Knights unlock the hidden crypt before Curston crumbles?

CURSE OF THE LOST GROVE

The Knights spend a night at the Lost Grove Inn. Can they discover the truth behind the inn's curse before it discovers them?

Ask for KNIGHTS OF THE SILVER DRAGON books at your favorite bookstore!

For ages eight to twelve

For more information visit www.mirrorstonebooks.com